EL DORADO COUNTY LIBRARY

3 1738 00844 7664

10

THE DAYSTAR VOYAGES

ATTACK OF THE DENEBIAN STARSHIP

GILBERT MORRIS
AND DAN MEEKS

D1016250

MOODY PRESS
CHICAGO

EL DORADO COUNTY LIBRARY
345 FAIR LANE
PLACERVILLE, CA 95667

©2000 by
GILBERT MORRIS
AND
DANIEL MEEKS

All rights reserved. No part of this book may be reproduced in any form without permission in writing from the publisher, except in the case of brief quotations embodied in critical articles or reviews.

All Scripture quotations, unless indicated, are taken from the *New American Standard Bible*, © 1960, 1962, 1963, 1968, 1971, 1972, 1973, 1975, 1977, and 1994 by The Lockman Foundation, La Habra, Calif. Used by permission.

ISBN: 0-8024-4114-9

1 3 5 7 9 10 8 6 4 2

Printed in the United States of America

To Mike McNair

I can't look at a bottle of Louisiana Hot Sauce without thinking of you. Thank you for being my friend and an encouraging, thoughtful, and insightful critic. I only hope that the years won't all go by until we can see each other again. I miss you.

—Dan

Characters

The *Daystar* ....an intergalactic star cruiser

The *Daystar* Space Rangers:
Jerusha Ericson, 15....a topflight engineer
Raina St. Clair, 14........the ship's communications
                            officer
Mei-Lani Lao, 13 ....*Daystar*'s historian and linguist
Ringo Smith, 14............a computer wizard
Heck Jordan, 15...........an electronics genius
Dai Bando, 16...............known for his exceptional
                            physical abilities

The *Daystar* Officers:
Mark Edge ....*Daystar*'s young captain
Zeno Thrax ....the first officer
Bronwen Llewellen ....the navigator; Dai's aunt
Temple Cole ....the flight surgeon
Ivan Petroski...............the chief engineer
Tara Jaleel ....the weapons officer
Studs Cagney ....the crew chief

Contents

1
Big Changes

Ever since Capt. Mark Edge recruited the *Daystar* Space Rangers for duty aboard his spaceship, they had been on many adventures. They had encountered many unusual—and often dangerous—events. But a wedding celebration—right on the edge of the most dangerous space in all of Intergalactic Command—was one thing none of them ever expected to see.

Command Base Three, located near the perilous Deneb sector, was one of Intergalactic Command's advanced guard posts. Command Base Three's very presence was a deterrent to any possible invasion threat of the Denebian Empire. The Denebians, every Ranger knew, were a ruthless people, likely to commit every kind of evil imaginable.

Six Magnum Deep Space Cruisers were assigned to this base, including the *Cromwell*, whose captain was Samantha Cook. Captain Cook was known as one of the sternest ship captains in the whole fleet. She always "went by the book." Never did the uncomplimentary term *ice queen* fit a person as well as the term fitted Captain Cook. Another thing could be said about her: She knew her crew inside and out.

Only two huge, heavy cruisers were connected to the docking ports today—the *Cromwell* and a visitor, the *Perseus*. The *Cromwell* was undergoing extensive repairs to its Star Drive engines, while the *Perseus* had come for an entirely different reason. The only other ship docked was the *Daystar*, which was dwarfed by the two larger vessels.

Normally, a military atmosphere prevailed at Command Base Three. The place was a kind of super-marine-corps post in outer space. Base personnel constantly kept on the alert for any unusual activity by the Denebians. Watchfulness was a way of life for those assigned to Command Base Three.

Today, though, was a different kind of day. Command Base Three was buzzing with activity. Something unusual was happening, and it was more than the wedding. While *Cromwell* was being repaired, the other five Magnum Deep Space Cruisers had been dispatched toward Deneb. The rumor mill was ablaze with guesses. Something was going on with the Denebians. So who would have thought there would be time for a wedding ceremony *now?*

But in spite of the frenzy, Commandant Winona Lee herself, the head of the Intergalactic Command Council, had made her appearance for the wedding ceremony. She was a small woman with silver gray hair and slate gray eyes. You couldn't have guessed her age to look at her. Today she was dressed in her formal Intergalactic Command uniform—a dark green tunic with gold braid on the collar and cuffs. She wore dark green pants that had a wide gold stripe running down the outside of each leg, and a pair of half boots that matched the color of her uniform. The most striking feature today, though, was her smile. She was beaming from ear to ear.

All of the Rangers and many other visitors as well had gathered on Command Base Three for Captain Edge's wedding. The Rangers had all been issued new uniforms. They were the military dress uniforms for ensigns who served full-time with the Intergalactic

Command Fleet. But each Ranger dreamed of the day when he or she would wear the dark green outfit that looked very much like Commandant Lee's, except for the gold braid and stripes.

During the moments just before the ceremony began, the Rangers stood together in a small group. Dai Bando, who at sixteen was the oldest Ranger, looked around at his friends. All of them, he saw, had worried looks on their faces.

Raina St. Clair appeared to be the most concerned. Raina was the communications expert. She was a petite girl with auburn hair. Her oval face had a dimple—which she said she hated—but at the moment the dimple did not show. And in fact, her green eyes looked very troubled. "I think this is *not* going to be a very happy wedding," she said.

Raina's close friend Mei-Lani Lao was standing beside her. Mei-Lani, the youngest of the Rangers, was Asian. She had jet black hair and warm brown eyes. At five feet one and only ninety-five pounds, she almost looked like a child among grownups. She was able to learn foreign languages the way most people learned the words to songs. Mei-Lani took Raina's arm and said, "It'll be all right. They'll be very happy together."

"Happy! How can you say a thing like that?" Heck Jordan popped a small candy bar into his mouth and began chewing. Heck was very overweight. In spite of the dress code, he had managed to ruin his appearance by wearing a pale pink-and-purple scarf. Since he was color-blind, he had no idea how awful this looked with his red hair. He mumbled around the candy bar. "Captain Edge is making a big mistake. A man loses his freedom when he gets married."

"I don't think Captain Edge sees it that way," Dai said. He smiled at Heck. "I think they'll be very happy together—and especially now since they both have decided to let Jesus be Lord of their lives. Dr. Cole loves the captain very much, and he loves her."

"That's plain to see," Ringo Smith joined in. Ringo always had a shy look about him, and a medallion always dangled around his neck—even today. On one side of it was a falcon and on the other side a strong-looking man. Until their trip to SharNu, he had thought the man was his father, Sir Richard Irons, one of the most vicious men in the entire galaxy. But there he'd learned that the image was of an earlier member of the Irons' family, a missionary who had brought Christianity to SharNu long ago. Ringo looked back at Dai. "They're both great people. They'll do all right."

Heck Jordan sniffed, and the others gave him disgusted looks.

"I think he's getting the best woman in the world for him," Mei-Lani said. "Dr. Cole is beautiful and smart and everything a woman ought to be, and she loves Captain Edge."

"You wouldn't have thought it when she first came on board," Jerusha said, smiling. "They fought like cats and dogs."

"But what I hate about it worst," Heck said, "is that they're going off on a honeymoon and then to some new assignment." He took out another candy bar. "That means we're going to get a new captain. And he'll probably be a real nerd."

"Why would you assume that, Heck?" Raina asked. "Command will likely give us another fine officer—just like Captain Edge."

"You can think that way if you want to, but I don't believe it. We'll probably get the worst captain in the whole intergalactic fleet."

"Oh, look, there they come now!" Mei-Lani cried. "Isn't Dr. Cole beautiful?"

Dai and the others all turned to the door and fixed their eyes on the bride.

Temple Cole was beautiful indeed. She had strawberry blonde hair, cut short, and violet eyes. She wore a white gown that seemed to shimmer from white to silver to lavender to pink as she walked. Her short veil was held in place by a white lace and pearl cap.

"I never saw her in anything but a uniform and medical smocks," Raina said. "She looks so different. And so beautiful."

"Just what a bride should look like," Jerusha said. "And see how handsome he is."

Dai knew Jerusha had once had a crush on the good-looking captain, but now she seemed truly happy for them both.

Captain Edge looked like one of the Vikings out of old Earth history. He had blond hair and blue-gray eyes and, as always, looked strong and alert. He was wearing a light blue uniform today. A red sash crossed his chest from shoulder to waist.

The ceremony itself was to be informal, and the smiling couple stopped on their way to the front. Dr. Cole said, "Look, Mark, here are all the *Daystar* babies."

Captain Edge laughed, and his white teeth flashed against his bronze skin. "I guess you could say that," he said. "Everyone always claimed I was running a nursery." But Dai heard the fondness in his voice.

Then Edge stopped smiling, and he studied their faces. "You don't look as happy as I'd like. What's up?"

"This is a happy day," Temple Cole said to the Rangers. "We're getting married. We want you to rejoice with us."

"Oh, we do," Jerusha said quickly. "We're all very happy for you."

"Yeah, we're just wondering what kind of a nerd we'll get for a captain," Heck blurted out.

"Heck, you needn't have a worry," Captain Edge said. "Intergalactic Command has a lot of capable captains to choose from."

Temple Cole shook her pretty head. "You always look at the dark side of things, Heck. I'm sure you'll be assigned a fine captain."

Then the captain took her arm. "Come along, sweetheart. They're waiting for us."

The two made their way on to the front, speaking to others along the way. And then the officer who was to conduct the ceremony, dressed in a pale green uniform, began to say the words.

From where Dai stood, a little to one side, he could watch the wedding and see the other Rangers as well. Their inner reactions were plain on their faces. Already, all three girls were crying. Dai himself was moved. He especially liked the part where the bride and groom pledged their loyalty to each other and to Jesus Christ. Heck was fidgeting around, as usual, and Ringo just looked down at the floor. But Dai was sure that every one of them—even Heck—was truly happy for Captain Edge and Dr. Cole.

In the middle of the ceremony, however, he could hear Heck muttering. "You watch what I tell you, Ringo. We're in for trouble."

"Will you shut up, Heck? This is a wedding!"

"No, I won't shut up. You never think ahead. That's your trouble."

Raina reached over and pinched his arm, hard. "Will you shush, Hector Jordan!" she whispered. "If you don't, I'll pinch a chunk out of you."

Heck gave her an offended look, then quieted down. But when the couple was leaving and everyone was throwing synthetic rice at them, he growled, "You all can say what you want, but you'll find out that I'm right. Old Heck is never wrong."

2
New Captain

The starship *Cromwell*, a Magnum Deep Space Cruiser, had been docked for extensive repairs and refitting. The *Cromwell* was finally being refitted with the new Mark V Star Drive engines. The old Mark IV engines had been in service for several years. The new Mark V's were designed to travel five hundred thousand light years without a tuneup. The *Cromwell* needed to catch up with the latest technology.

While they were replacing the engines, Intergalactic Command decided to install the latest artificial intelligence computers aboard the ship, too. So, when information began to come in about suspicious activity among the Denebians, *Cromwell*'s captain had to sit idly by at Command Base Three because the *Cromwell* was in the midst of repairs.

Capt. Samantha Cook—known as Sam to some— was upset by the timing of everything. She could not bear just sitting and doing nothing. Captain Cook had to be in space.

After she had voiced her dissatisfaction on several occasions, she was called in by her superiors. She would be given command of the *Daystar*, they said. Captain Edge was going on his honeymoon, they said, and would be reassigned a new ship upon his return. Captaining the *Daystar* was not to Samantha Cook's liking—she was a difficult captain to please—but commanding a small cruiser was better than just sitting around doing nothing.

As she looked at the *Daystar* at the docking port, she felt uncomfortable. It was a feeling that seemed to plague her these days. *Why do I keep having this sense of foreboding?* Cook asked herself over and over. *Whatever is coming, I have to be prepared for it. This crew has to be prepared for it.*

Captain Cook approached the *Daystar*, putting determination into her every step. "I know I'll have to whip this crew into shape," she muttered. "I never had any use for Mark Edge's relaxed methods. He was nothing but an ex-pirate himself."

Captain Cook was no longer young. She was very tall for a woman, slightly more than five eleven. It was said that her icy gray eyes could freeze junior officers, and her lips ordinarily were one thin line. She wore her long blonde hair in a braid down to the small of her back. Her life was the space fleet.

Captain Cook walked through the portal of the *Daystar*, and a whistle sounded. A voice blared over the speaker system, "Captain coming aboard! Captain coming aboard!"

The *Daystar* came alive with the officers and the Rangers and the rest of the crew hurrying to the chow hall. The eating area was the largest room aboard the cruiser, so it also was used as an assembly room and rec hall.

Dai watched with the rest as a tall, businesslike woman with cold eyes entered.

The crew chief, Studs Cagney, stood next to Dai. Studs saw her and groaned. "Oh no, it's Sam Cook!"

"Who is she?" Tara Jaleel whispered. The weapons officer was a tall woman of Masai stock, well over six feet and with fierce features.

"You'll find out," Cagney groaned. "Life will be miserable from now on."

Zeno Thrax, the albino first officer, may have been rather chilling to look at, but he really was of a mild disposition. He murmured, "We'll just have to get along with her, Studs."

Everyone came to attention at Thrax's order, and Captain Cook took her place on a small platform. From that vantage point, she would be able to see every face. She let her eyes go over the entire group, and it was obvious that she was all business.

"I'm Capt. Samantha Cook. I've been assigned by the Council to assume command of this ship." She paused for one moment, and again her eyes went from face to face. It was plain to see that this woman did not believe in coddling anyone. She wanted at the very outset to get this clearly in the minds of the crew.

"None of you have ever served under me, and I think it's well that you understand right now that I am not running a nursery here."

Dai watched her eyes fly to the youthful Space Rangers, and he understood at once that they would be on trial.

"I will be fair, but all of you will have to earn your positions. You had a captain that you served, but he is gone, and now you will become accustomed to a new way of doing things."

"I'd rather charge a Denebian outpost," Studs whispered to Zeno.

Total silence ran over the room then. Dai guessed that every officer knew they were all in for a difficult time. The crew knew it. The Space Rangers certainly knew it.

And then Ivan Petroski, the chief engineer, mut-

17

tered his opinion—too loudly. "This is going to be a real picnic, this is!"

At once Captain Cook's eyes fixed on the dwarf who capably served as chief engineer. "What is your name and rank?" she rapped out.

"Petroski. Engineer, Captain."

"This crew will keep its mouth shut when I am speaking! Do you understand that?"

"Yes, Captain," Petroski growled and clamped his lips shut.

"I have spent the last few days poring over your personal files. All of you have strengths and weaknesses." Captain Cook tugged down the front of her green tunic, making her look even more trim and fit. "During the next few days I will be testing your skills in various ways," she said sternly. "You will all be expected to perform at top level. Dismissed!" the captain said, and she marched out of the chow hall.

"Wow!" Ringo breathed. He looked totally depressed. "It looks like we've gotten ourselves a real dinger this time."

"I told you so," Heck said. "But never mind. I'll turn on the old charm. You guys know that women of all ages can't resist me."

"If you do that," Raina said bleakly, "she'll probably throw you out the hatch into space."

Dai had kept silent until now. Although Captain Cook sounded tough, he somehow sensed that meanness was not her real intent. He looked over at Heck and Raina. "It won't be so bad," he said. "We all know our jobs."

However, Dai Bando's words did not come true. Actually, he was the first one to run into trouble. After their shakedown flight with the new captain, the very first duty change that Captain Cook made was to assign Dai to the main computer controls.

"I believe that's a mistake, Captain," Zeno Thrax said, still feeling shock at the news. "Dai Bando is an excellent ensign, but his strength doesn't lie in technology, Captain. Even a small computer is very difficult for him, and you have placed him in main computer control. That's an accident waiting to happen—sir!"

"Are you questioning my orders, Thrax?"

"Well, I thought you might like my opinion. I've been with these young people a long time—"

"You will keep your opinions to yourself, Thrax! I will make my own decisions."

"Yes, Captain."

Zeno left the captain's station and went to look for Dai Bando. He found the boy helping Studs Cagney shift boxes. This was exactly the sort of thing that he did well.

Dai turned to the first officer and listened to his new orders.

"But—but I don't know how to do that, sir."

"You'll have to do the best you can," Thrax said. "I'll stand by all I can to give you what help I can."

Studs Cagney heard all of this and became so angry that he stomped over and spit into the trash bin. "Women officers," Studs sneered. "They're nothing but trouble."

Zeno patted Studs on the shoulder. "Give her a chance. That's all we can do."

It turned out that it was impossible to give young Dai help. He was placed in charge of Main Computer Control, and Captain Cook said sternly, "You will operate the ship by yourself, Bando."

Thrax and Tara Jaleel, who stood watching, gave each other despairing looks. They both knew that for all of his fine qualities, Dai Bando's strength was not in

19

this sort of thing. It took only ten minutes before Dai made a serious mistake. The ship's computer alarm sounded loudly, and Captain Cook—she probably had been waiting for this—moved in quickly. She made adjustments to the controls and then turned on him. "Bando," she said, "you're worthless! You nearly caused the ship to self-destruct!"

Dai Bando did not respond but stood there calmly.

"Put him to work with the grunts."

"Yes, Captain," Zeno said. He led Dai Bando off to the cargo bay to find the crew chief.

When Studs Cagney heard what had happened, he said, "Good enough. You stay with me, Dai. The farther you're away from that woman, the better."

Dai Bando did not usually complain, but he had always felt he was different from the other Rangers. They all had highly technical skills, while all he had was his strength, his speed, and his courage. Now he went about his business helping Studs.

It was late in the afternoon when Bronwen Llewellen, who was his aunt and also the navigator of the *Daystar*, sought him out. Bronwen Llewellen was an older lady with silver hair. She had been a space pioneer. In fact, she had more experience as a navigator than anyone else in the fleet. She came into the cargo hold and put a hand on his shoulder. "I heard, Dai. Don't worry about it," she said.

"I'm not really worried, Aunt Bronwen. I'm just trying to understand her. I sense that deep down the captain is not as mean as she wants us to believe. But why does she have to act that way?"

"She's a strange woman," Bronwen said. "She's read all the crew's personality files, and now it seems she's trying to point out weaknesses."

"But *everybody* has weaknesses—even our new captain herself."

"Yes, but I'm afraid Captain Cook is going to make our weaknesses seem even worse than they are."

Jerusha Ericson had one love outside of her job on *Daystar*, and that was her dog, Contessa. Contessa was a superbred German shepherd, large, black, and highly intelligent. She was also strong and a fierce threat to anyone who threatened Jerusha.

Captain Cook no doubt had watched this carefully. One day, the dog became caught in an airlock that vented air into space. Cook, who was standing a short distance away, electronically shut the door, and then the outside hatch started to open.

Jerusha took in all this at a glance and began running. She knew that if she opened the inner hatch, then the whole cargo bay might be sucked into space, but there was nothing else to do to save the dog. She opened the inner hatch. Immediately the outer hatch closed tightly.

At that moment Captain Cook stepped forward from where she had been watching the whole thing. "Ericson, you're a sorry officer!"

"Why . . . why do you say that, Captain?"

"You allowed your love for that animal to cloud your judgment!"

Jerusha knew she had done exactly that, but she also thought that the captain was being terribly unfair. She knew very well that Captain Cook had organized the test and had risked Contessa's life. However, she also knew that to speak up would be fatal. So she left after being dismissed, knowing that she had failed her test.

Ringo heard about Dai's and Jerusha's experiences, and he was sure that his turn was coming. He was not mistaken. The very night after Jerusha lost status with the captain, Captain Cook approached Ringo and said, "Smith, you will be on the bridge tonight. By yourself."

"Yes, Captain."

Ringo had stood watches before but never with quite so much responsibility. He determined to let nothing go wrong. Actually, he was a very uncertain boy. There was his father's being a pirate, and Ringo felt a burden of guilt because of that. The son of a ruthless pirate was nothing to be proud about. In addition, he was just naturally shy and had always had trouble making decisions. For these reasons he was determined not to fail.

The hours passed quietly, and nothing happened. Then, suddenly, alarms were sounding everywhere. The gauges told him that the Star Drive cooling system had ruptured, the life support system had shut down, and an explosion had taken place in the cargo bay. Ringo knew what to do when things happened one at a time, but now everything was going wrong at once!

He ran around wildly, not knowing what to do first. In his confusion he did nothing.

After perhaps sixty seconds of this, Captain Cook marched onto the bridge.

"Captain, I'm glad you're here!" Ringo cried.

Cook gave him a disgusted look. "Computer, stop simulation!"

Instantly, every gauge returned to normal, and Ringo realized then that it had all been a test. Nothing had been actually happening.

"You're on first probation!" Captain Cook declared.

"But—but, Captain, that's not fair!"

Captain Cook gave him a harsh look and said clearly, "Life is testing us every day, Smith. You've got

22

to make decisions instantly. The lives of this ship and this crew depend on the ability to make decisions in crisis situations, and you failed!"

Ringo could not meet her cold eyes. "I'm sorry, Captain," he whispered.

"You may be sorry, but that doesn't change the fact that the ship would have been demolished if you had been in control."

"Yes, Captain."

Ringo left the bridge and went at once to his cabin, where he sat down on his bunk. He drew up his legs and put his arms around his knees, holding them tightly. Putting his head down, he struggled with his emotions.

A soft knock came, and he muttered, "Come in."

Raina stepped inside and took one look. Then she sat down on the bunk and put her arm around Ringo. "I heard about it," she said.

"It was awful."

"I know it was, but you've got to get over it, Ringo."

"What does she want out of us!" he exclaimed. He lifted his head. "I'm doing the very best I can."

"She's determined to fail all of us. She failed Jerusha, and she failed Dai, and now she's failed you. My turn will probably be next."

"How does she think this is going to help make a good ship? We did our jobs fine with Captain Edge. He said so."

Raina thought about that, then said, "I believe she's really envious of Captain Edge."

"She's sure not as good a captain as he is."

"Well, she may be *technically*—but she doesn't know how to get along with people the way Captain Edge does. Don't tell anyone, but I've been making a few inquiries about her on the computer."

"Raina, you could get into big trouble for doing that." He sat up straight and looked at her with his forehead wrinkled.

"I know," Raina said. "But I learned she's never been able to get along with people. She's determined to be in command, and she's totally intolerant of any weakness she finds in another person."

"Well, why doesn't she look at herself? I bet she's got plenty of weaknesses."

"I think she's built a wall around herself, Ringo. Don't worry. It'll all work out."

"It's working out rotten so far."

It was clear to Ringo that Raina wanted to comfort him, but he was totally miserable.

"We've got to stick together, Ringo," she said grimly. "I'm sure there's only worse to come."

"Worse! How could it be worse?"

"It can always be worse. But right now, you come along with me."

"Come where?"

"Down to the rec room. We're going to play a game of Dorisian battle chess, and I'm going to beat your socks off."

Raina would not take no for an answer, and after a few lively games, Ringo was thinking, *Well, I guess this is cheering me up. But Raina's probably right. Her turn is coming.*

3
Secret Orders

The Space Rangers were not the only ones tested by the new captain. She proceeded to make life miserable for others as well, including Crew Chief Studs Cagney and Chief Engineer Ivan Petroski. Both were excellent officers and had proved their worth over and over, but as the *Daystar* plowed through space, Captain Cook found a way to make even the two of them look terrible.

Captain Cook's plan for testing Studs and Ivan was very simple—she ordered them to exchange jobs. Studs was virtually lost in Engineering, and Ivan's temper almost caused the grunts to mutiny. Ivan ran as fast as his short legs could carry him while he breathed out threats at every crewman in sight. It was only because of Dai's presence in the cargo bay that Petroski didn't find himself strung up from the ceiling. Dai had never seen the grunts so angry.

When Captain Cook reviewed the men's performance at their new assignments, she belittled them to the point of humiliation. She ordered them to return to their usual jobs and dismissed them with a wave of her hand. Captain Edge had never treated them this way.

"I wish that woman would step outside into space and never be seen again," Cagney groaned. "We never do anything right."

Ivan Petroski's eyes were hard with anger. "All she succeeds in doing is humiliating people. This is going to be a bad flight, Studs."

"What would happen if she got so bad we had to override her orders?"

Petroski looked around quickly. "Hush up! Don't say such things! That's mutiny talk."

Studs Cagney was a rough, tough sort of fellow with thinning black hair and dark eyes. He was short and muscular and had been a rough, brutal, self-confident man. Ever since Dai Bando had come onto the ship, however, Studs had been somewhat puzzled. There was something about Dai Bando's Christian character that intrigued him.

He sighed. "Well, I've never mutinied yet," he said, "and I don't reckon I'll start now."

Up on the bridge Zeno Thrax and Tara Jaleel were having a hushed conversation. Jaleel's eyes glittered with anger. "That woman had better be careful! I'll report her to Intergalactic Command—that is, after I smash her against the bulkhead!"

Zeno Thrax gave his fellow officer a cautious glance. "Intergalactic Command doesn't like officers criticizing their captains. And they would really frown on you manhandling Captain Cook. You could wind up in the brig for the next fifty years."

"I don't care what they like! She's not a good officer."

"The records show different," Thrax said mildly. "She has very successfully completed many dangerous missions. In fact, Cook has the highest evaluation score of any captain in the fleet with the exception of Captain Pursey, who commands Intergalactic's flagship."

"I'd like to know what her former crew on the *Cromwell* was like," Jaleel replied. "She doesn't have a friend on *this* ship."

"I don't think she wants any," Thrax said. "She's a strange woman. Never been married and, from what I hear, never wanted to be. Her whole life's purpose seems to be to advance in rank in fleet command."

"She'll never make it," Jaleel said bitterly.

"She might," Zeno said quietly. "The Council thrives on success, and sometimes they're not too careful about how it comes."

At that moment Raina St. Clair called out, "Commander Thrax, new orders coming over."

Thrax crossed to where Raina sat before the communications board.

"These are secret orders, only for the captain's eyes," Raina said.

"Then send them at once to her office," the first officer ordered.

Raina obeyed, and soon everyone aboard the *Daystar* knew that something was up.

"Those secret orders mean something's going on," Heck Jordan said, walking into Ringo Smith's work area.

Ringo had become good friends with Heck, in spite of their many differences. Heck was an outgoing boy, even arrogant at times. He truly was an electronics expert. But he had delusions about his own abilities, and he still irritated people greatly. Even Ringo.

Pulling a pack of jellybeans out of his pocket, Heck searched until he found some black ones. Then he began to munch on them. "I'll bet it's big trouble," he said.

"We don't know that," Ringo said. "It could all be routine."

"That's what I hate about you." Heck grinned. "You always look on the good side of things. I love pessimists."

Ringo managed a grin himself, and then suddenly the captain's voice crackled over the intercom. "All officers to the conference room."

"That's us. Come on," Heck said.

The conference area was also known as the war room. The officers gathered about a large, white, oval table.

Like everyone else, Ringo was tense. And like everyone else, when Captain Cook came in, he kept his eyes fixed on her.

The captain took one look at the white table and shook her head as though disgusted. "Be seated," she said.

"Obviously she doesn't like white," Zeno whispered to Bronwen Llewellen as the officers seated themselves about the table.

"We have received orders," Captain Cook announced crisply. "And news. A large Denebian starship has destroyed the *Jackray.*"

Ringo gasped. His father had been commander of the *Jackray.* Sir Richard may have been a vicious man, who had never shown the least affection for his son, but still he had been Ringo's only living relative. At once he felt every eye turn to him.

Captain Cook looked around the war room, seeming mystified by the total silence. "What's wrong?"

"What about Sir Richard Irons, Captain?" Bronwen Llewellen asked. "The *Jackray*'s commander. You may not have known, but Ringo Smith is his son."

Captain Cook turned to Ringo and studied him coldly for a long moment. "No, I didn't know that. But in any case, all hands were killed instantly." The captain didn't show the least concern that Ringo had just heard that his father was dead.

"Somehow," she went on, "the Denebians sneaked

into our territory without our long-range beacons sensing them. We don't know what Irons was doing in the area, but he apparently drew their attention. And, as all of you should know, it's a dangerous thing to draw the Denebians' attention. In fact, the word that comes to mind is 'deadly'!"

The young Space Rangers and the *Daystar*'s older officers still sat looking stunned at the news they had just heard. Captain Cook understood their shock. The "most dangerous man in the galaxy" had been wiped out, suddenly and without warning.

Then Jerusha said quietly, "I'm so very sorry, Ringo."

"A tough break," Heck murmured.

And the others began making their murmurs of sympathy.

Captain Cook noticed the compassion that was being shown to Ringo Smith. For once, she displayed uncertainty. She had followed the career of Irons carefully, as had all other star fleet captains. She knew that he had been one of the galaxy's biggest dangers. For that reason she was relieved that he was gone. But, studying young Smith's face, she saw how upset he was. "Were you very close to your father, then?" she asked.

The boy seemed unable to think clearly. "Uh . . . no, Captain . . . not at all. In fact, for some reason, he . . . he hated me . . . he meant to do me harm. I know that. Don't worry about me." Ringo looked up into her eyes, then back down at the table. "My father was really a stranger to me."

"Ringo," the navigator said, "I guess this makes you Sir Ringo Irons, the new ruler of Palenque. Sooner or later your life could be taking a dramatic change."

But Tara Jaleel interrupted that line of thought. "I think we should relieve Ringo Smith of his duties in a case like this," she said loudly.

"He has duties to carry out," Cook snapped back, "and if he can't handle them, he has no business on a star cruiser! And he's not a ruler yet—he's a member of this crew with duties to perform."

Bronwen Llewellen glanced about at the other officers' faces. The harshness of Captain Cook's reply was obviously revolting to everyone.

Even Tara Jaleel, who had no special affection for any of the Space Rangers, acted disgusted. "It's common practice, Captain," she said crisply, "when someone has lost a relative, to relieve them for a time."

"Not on my ship!"

Bronwen Llewellen was a gentle woman, but she decided she must speak up in behalf of Ringo. "I think you might want to reconsider that, Captain Cook—if for no other reason than for the efficiency of the ship. Anyone suffering the loss of a close family member will not be able to work at the top of his ability."

"I expect my officers to function well under any circumstances!"

"But this is different!" Jerusha cried. "You can't expect—"

"I'll have no more discussion of this! The issue is settled!" Captain Cook glared around defiantly. "Some of you are going to have to learn what discipline means! We are going into battle, and it may be the one sitting right next to you who dies. What will you do then? Take a vacation from your duties? I won't have it! We're going to obey orders no matter what happens." The tone of Cook's voice confirmed to the navigator that she was totally serious. Her mind was made up.

Anyone could see that it was hopeless, and it was Ringo himself who said, "I'm all right, Captain. Really."

"That's better!" Cook touched a button, and a star chart suddenly appeared on the opposite wall. Then she took a laser pointer from her belt.

"The Denebian starship—" she began, as the brilliant dot traveled over the chart. "It is headed toward the southeast quadrant, according to the latest information we have at Command Base Three." There was a puzzled note in the captain's voice as she went on. "I can't imagine what the Denebians want in that quadrant."

Although that section of the galaxy was hardly explored, it was generally believed that nothing of value was located there. The robot drones that had been sent into the area reported only arid worlds, possibly with heavy gravity that would be uncomfortable for people from Earth.

But Bronwen Llewellen—indeed all those who had been on the *Daystar* for some time—knew exactly what was in that quadrant. Before he had become an Intergalactic Command captain, Mark Edge had visited a small planet called Makon in that area. On that planet, he had found traces of a crystal—tridium—so valuable that it could make its owner master of the galaxy. Edge was unable to do more than obtain a small sample. But Sir Richard Irons learned of Edge's discovery and he too had sought to find the location of the planet.

Bronwen considered telling all of this to the new captain, but she still did not entirely trust Captain Cook. Also she was not sure that Intergalactic Command would want that information to be disclosed. So, instead, Bronwen decided to break the silence by saying, "Captain, can you tell us what you know about the Denebians and what battle strategies they use?" She wanted to move the subject safely away from the tridium.

Cook's right eye squinted half closed as she looked back at Bronwen. "Well, Navigator, if my memory serves me right, and it does, you are one of the few people in Intergalactic Command to have visited the Deneb star system and lived to tell about it." The captain paced around the white conference table and sat down in the captain's chair. "*You* tell us."

Bronwen got up and approached the star chart. "I do have some information," she said. "Some of you have heard this before, so forgive me for the repetition."

Heck muttered thoughtfully, "Be careful, Bronwen. This could be your test."

Captain Cook didn't take her eyes off Bronwen as she snarled, "Ensign Jordan, one more word out of you and I'll use you as bait for our Denebian friends out there."

Bronwen smiled slightly at Heck and shook her head from side to side before turning back to the chart.

"That means 'shut up' in Bronwen-ese, in case you don't get it," Ringo muttered to Heck.

Bronwen picked up the laser pointer and made a circular motion on the chart. "This is the Cygnus sector." She moved the pointer to one side and stopped on a large bright dot. "This star is Deneb. It marks the top of the Northern Cross as seen from Earth over eighteen hundred light years away. Most people aren't aware of this, but Earth's solar system is racing toward Deneb at a speed of two hundred fifty kilometers per second."

"Whew!" Ivan exclaimed. "Any sane person would want to run in the opposite direction, and Earth is headed right for it?"

Bronwen chuckled. "If it's any comfort, we won't be anywhere near Deneb for millions of years yet. The galaxy is a pretty big place." Bronwen backed up a couple of steps. "Deneb is a supergiant star of spectral type A2 Ia."

"What does that mean, Bronwen?" Mei-Lani asked.

"Oh, I've read about that," Jerusha broke in. "It means that Deneb is one of the brightest stars in the galaxy. Ancient Earth astronomers designated Deneb as A2 because it's a blue-white star with a temperature range somewhere between seventy-five hundred and ten thousand degrees. The 'Ia' just means it's a bright supergiant."

"Correct." Bronwen said. "There is much we still don't know about Deneb. Intergalactic Command scientists report that there are strange ionic emissions that radiate throughout the Denebian solar system."

She magnified the chart to display the Deneb star system. "As you can see, all the planets of the Deneb system glow with an iridescent greenish color." Bronwen turned to the table. "Imagine living in a world where everything—land, water, and sky—is green."

"I don't know, Bronwen. It doesn't look very green to me," Heck remarked.

Raina reached over and pulled at Heck's purple scarf. "Ssh. That's because you're color-blind. Would you be quiet?"

Cook ignored Heck and studied the Deneb solar system. "And what about the Denebians themselves, Navigator?"

"History databases don't tell us much. It's thought that the Denebians are descendants of the Nishka." Bronwen leaned back against the bulkhead while she continued. "The Nishka were a people who had remarkable abilities. Nishka warriors rarely lost battles." She smiled at Weapons Officer Tara Jaleel. "They had a unique ability and used it to their advantage."

"What ability was that?" Studs asked. A Denebian

starship was on the loose, and he acted eager to learn all he could.

"It was the ability to somehow affect others with terror—whether a single person or a whole race. They destroyed many civilizations that way—including the Amesstorites, who were one of the most noble races to exist in intergalactic history."

"So the Denebians are actually descended from the Nishka?" Raina asked.

"As I said, that's the popular thought."

Heck interrupted with, "Well, if the Denebians are really the Nishka descendants, why don't they just call themselves Nishka?"

"We really don't know," Bronwen answered.

"You've told quite a good story up till now, Navigator. In any case, whoever they are descended from, I don't think the Denebians are afraid of anything except our turbo cannons!" Captain Cook said.

Bronwen looked back at the star chart. "One thing we do know about them for sure is that they destroyed the Amesstorites. Without that great race to protect this quadrant of space, the Nishka were free to destroy every other race left in existence."

"What happened?" Raina said just loud enough for Bronwen to hear.

"This is the mysterious part that's hinted at on the databases. An intergalactic fleet, from parts unknown, overcame the Nishka themselves—except for the ones that fled into Deneb space. It is the descendants of those refugees that we know as the Denebians today."

"Who were the conquerors?" Ringo asked.

"Intergalactic Command doesn't know their name, but we do have record of the crest that was on their ships." Bronwen walked around to Ringo and took his medallion in her hand. "A bird of prey and the face of a man—just like what is on Ringo's medallion. Ringo, through the Irons family, is a descendent of this mysterious race. The Irons family knows little of its ancient past, but they were a noble people, Ringo. Even if Sir Richard himself was evil, his ancestors—your ancestors—were a great people, who spread the gospel to many corners of the galaxy."

Heck laughed. "And here I've been buddies with royalty all this time and didn't know it."

Chuckles filled the room but were brought to a quick halt when Captain Cook's fist slammed the top of the conference table. "Enough of this." The captain was now as serious as Bronwen had ever seen her. "Navigator," Cook said, more respectfully this time, "tell us what else you know about the Denebians."

"The Denebians are the most ruthless race to live in our time. We don't know if that's because of the green radiation in their solar system, or because they're descendants of the Nishka, or for some other reason. The Denebians have destroyed whole worlds. No one in Intergalactic Command truly knows the strength of their weapons. They take no prisoners, and they give no quarter once they engage the enemy." Bronwen returned to her chair. "Captain, the last thing we want to do is engage the Denebians in a war. Millions of lives would be lost."

Captain Cook stood up then and walked around the conference room to the star chart. "Commandant Lee has given us our orders. Intergalactic Command knows that the Denebian ship is headed for this quadrant." She indicated the Makon sector with the laser pointer. "We are to discover the whereabouts of the Denebian starship and then send a report to Intergalactic Command when we are out of range. Being a small cruiser, the *Daystar* might be ignored by the Denebians."

The captain looked around the war room. Everyone was quiet. Bronwen Llewellen's history lesson had
just turned into harsh reality. "Very well. We have our
orders. Everyone get to your stations. Be prepared."

As they left, Heck said to any Ranger who was listening, "Well, that'll take care of this stupid testing,
anyhow."

4

New Assignment

The *Daystar* shot through space with her Mark V Star Drive engines purring like a kitten. Ivan Petroski loved the *Daystar*. No expense of time or money had been spared to improve the very heart of the ship—the engines—*his* engines. Being a small man, Ivan was able to personally inspect and correct problems that average-sized adults couldn't get to.

As Petroski glanced out the portal in Engineering, he saw the familiar sight of stars rushing by. He knew this was an illusion, of course. The stars hardly moved, according to human standards of time and space. It was *Daystar* that was rushing forward into the unknown . . . into great danger . . . into possible destruction. Ivan well knew that to be a great engineer aboard a star cruiser, you must love your engines. More than that, you must be willing to sacrifice the very thing that you love. Ivan was willing.

Heck Jordan was totally convinced that, with the crisis concerning the Denebian starship, Captain Cook would forget about testing the rest of the crew. He even bragged about it to Raina. He found her in the rec room and plopped himself down beside her. "Well, it looks like the captain is going to be human for a while."

Raina looked doubtful. "I wouldn't be too sure about that, Heck."

"Why wouldn't you be sure?"

"Because she's a very determined woman."

"Determined or not, we're heading toward a battle. She won't be fooling around with tests."

Raina shook her head and took a sip of her nectar juice. "I hope you're right."

"Depend on it," Heck said with a big smile and a quick wink.

He patted Raina's arm and grinned in what he thought was a charming manner. "When we get back home, maybe the two of us could go out and see the town, Raina. Have a celebration."

"We'll see," she said, just a little sarcastically.

"Sure. We'll see."

At that moment, the loudspeaker came alive. "Hector Jordan, report to the captain's office."

Raina gave him a troubled look. "Watch yourself, Heck."

"Ah, she just wants to tell me what a good job I've been doing." He grinned.

Heck made his way confidently down the corridor until he reached the captain's office. He spoke and waited for a moment, and then the panel opened. He found Capt. Samantha Cook seated at her desk. "Ensign Jordan reporting, Captain."

"I've been studying your records, Ensign," Captain Cook said. She glanced up at him, and there was a hard look in her eyes. "I'm afraid they're not satisfactory."

"Not satisfactory! Why, I'm the best electronics man in the star fleet!"

"You've done some things rather well. And in some ways you have been excellent in your innovations. But you have absolutely no discipline, Jordan."

Heck began to argue.

He was interrupted at once by the captain's loud voice. "You have no discipline! Look at you! You're sixty pounds overweight. Captain Edge assigned you

38

to do martial arts with Lieutenant Jaleel, and you've not followed orders."

"I hate that stuff. I'll never have to fight anybody," he protested.

"You don't know what you'll have to do, Ensign Jordan, and you've violated Captain Edge's orders. Well, you won't violate mine!"

"No, sir, of course not!" Captain Cook frightened Heck somehow. She had a look in her eyes that he didn't like. "I'll do much better, Captain," he promised.

"Yes, you will. I'll see to that."

"Uh . . . may I go now, Captain?"

"No, you may not go! Here are my orders. You will eat nothing except vegetables, a small amount of fruit, and two slices of bread per meal. You will drink nothing but water."

"But, Captain, I'll die!"

"You won't die. You may lose some of that excess weight. You understand my orders clearly?"

"Yes, Captain, but—"

"Do you understand that if you are caught eating anything except what I have ordered, you will be placed under arrest for a violation of captain's orders?"

Heck was sure he turned pale. He could only nod.

"Empty your pockets!"

"I beg your pardon?"

"Empty your pockets!"

Heck knew exactly what Captain Cook was getting at. He slowly began to empty his pockets onto her desk. When he had finished, there was a mound of small chocolate bars, jelly beans, licorice whips, bags of peanuts, and half a sandwich that he had saved from the last meal.

"Disgusting!" Captain Cook sniffed. "You will be under observation, and I have informed Lieutenant

Jaleel that you will spend at least two hours a day doing physical fitness work and practicing martial arts."

This was worse than anything Heck had imagined. He wanted to beg for mercy, but he could see that was useless. When the captain finally said, "That's all. You may leave," he turned and left her office on wobbly legs. He found that he was perspiring. He went straight down the corridor to Ringo's station in the computer room and plunked himself down.

"I'm going to die!" he gasped.

Alarmed, Ringo looked up. "What's the matter? You having a heart attack?"

"I'm going to."

Ringo got up and came over to Heck. "I'll call for the medical officer," he said in a concerned voice.

"It won't do any good."

"What's wrong with you, Heck?"

"Do you know what that crazy captain has done to me?"

"No, I don't. What is it?"

"She says I can't have anything to eat except vegetables, fruit, and two slices of bread at every meal—and no soda pops. Nothing but water!"

"She said that?"

"Yes. And that's not all. She said I had to spend two hours a day exercising, and everyone knows that Lieutenant Jaleel is going to kill me in those martial arts lessons."

Ringo peered into Heck's face. Then he put a hand on his shoulder. "Maybe it won't be so bad."

"Won't be bad! I'll starve to death, and what's left of me will be crunched by Lieutenant Jaleel. You know how *she* is."

Ringo looked sympathetic. He seemed to be trying

40

to think of something comforting to say. Everybody knew that Lieutenant Jaleel was merciless in her teaching of the martial arts. Ringo had his own share of bruises.

"Well, we'll be going into action pretty soon," he said at last. "Then her mind will be on other things."

"You don't know that woman! Captain Cook is awful! Right in the middle of a battle, if she caught me eating one single candy bar, she'd probably have me shot."

"Oh, it's not that bad, Heck," Ringo said.

"You just don't know. You don't understand."

Ringo spent some time trying to calm Heck down, but nothing he said seemed to do much good. When his shift was over, he headed for the rec area, where he found Jerusha.

She listened and nodded. "It's about the kind of thing I'd expect Captain Cook to do. She's studied all of our shortcomings, and she knows that the love of food is one of Heck's greatest flaws." Jerusha seemed in deep thought as she tapped the table with her fingers. "We've known Heck for a long time, Ringo. This kind of diet will drive Heck crazy. And if he's crazy, he'll drive the rest of us crazy, too."

Ringo was in full agreement. "Do you think we could get someone to talk to her? I mean, after all, we all know that Heck needs to eat less, but this crash program might be bad for him. And you know how he hates being beat up by Lieutenant Jaleel."

"I don't think talking to anybody would do any good," Jerusha said quietly. "We're just going to have to endure it."

Heck Jordan had never been so miserable in all his life. The captain had given strict orders that anyone see-

41

ing him eat anything except at mealtime was to report it. He was certain that none of his friends would do that, but there were new crew members who were not his friends and who were frightened of the captain. He was shocked when Captain Cook even ordered Zeno Thrax to personally see that no food of any kind was in Heck's cabin. Thrax had been apologetic, but he had said, "Those are orders, Heck. I don't have any choice."

Thrax had done an excellent job with those orders, and for two days Heck had eaten less than he had in years. The few small candy bars that he had stashed away were all gone, and now there was nothing.

He sat before the computer, staring at it listlessly. It was late at night. His stomach was growling, and he felt hungry enough to eat cotton.

"I've got to have something to eat," he moaned.

He considered going to the other Rangers and asking them to scrounge some food for him.

He had already tried that, however, and it didn't work. All had said his "diet" was good for him and that, although it would be tough for a time, he would be better when he had slimmed down and was in good shape.

The silence ran on. Only the humming of the computers disturbed the room.

"I've got to have something to eat!" he muttered again. Then Heck had a crafty thought.

He got up and tiptoed down the central corridor. He looked carefully into the galley and finally was convinced that no one was inside. Slipping in, he shut the door and began to look around. Food was easily obtained here. Usually, he thought, someone was on duty. But tonight there was no one!

Heck loaded a plate with pie and cake and began eating hungrily. However, he had taken no more than a few bites when the galley door opened. He stood aghast as Captain Cook entered and stood before him, triumph in her eyes. Heck tried to conceal the plate, but he knew his mouth was smeared with chocolate.

"I warned you what would happen, didn't I?"

"But, Captain, I'm starving!"

"Consider yourself confined to quarters! You will be locked inside and released only when you will be on duty. During duty, you will be monitored at all times."

"But, Captain—"

"You heard my orders!"

Miserably Heck slumped his shoulders. Then he dragged himself out of the galley, licking his lips for the last bit of sweetness. When he went into his room, he heard the door close behind him with a final-sounding click.

He threw himself on his bed, utterly woebegone. Maybe he *was* a little selfish at times, he thought, but he did not feel that he deserved what was happening to him. In spite of himself, Heck felt a choking in his throat, and he wanted to cry. He did not, however. Instead he muttered, "I will live through this. I will live through this. And I'll get the best of Captain Cook, yet. See if I don't!"

Mei-Lani was disturbed about Heck. She considered going to the captain, and she talked with Raina and Ringo about it. But then all three of them decided that would be useless. Besides, something was warning Mei-Lani that she herself would not be left out of Captain Cook's testing.

As it happened, the very next day after Heck's downfall, Captain Cook called Mei-Lani into her office. "Lao, I'm reassigning you to Engineering."

"Engineering! But, sir, I'm the historian, the linguist!"

"You are responsible for any duty that I give you. Now, that's all."

"Captain Cook, you're making a mistake!"

"Did you hear my orders? You're dismissed!"

Mei-Lani tried to reason with her, but she soon saw that was hopeless. She started back to her cabin and was met on the way by Ivan Petroski. "I just got the word, Mei-Lani," he said. "You're to be in Engineering."

"I don't know anything about engineering!"

"That woman is going to wreck this ship," Petroski said grimly. "You'll just have to do the best you can. I'll help as much as I can."

Mei-Lani assumed her new duties and indeed did the best she could. But she knew it was only a matter of time before disaster struck.

It was now her duty to monitor the life support system, and at first everything seemed fine. But then the cruiser jolted fiercely as if under attack. Flames erupted from several places, blocking her from reaching the vital controls needed for the safety of the ship.

Terrified, Mei-Lani started to run through the blaze to reach the controls, but she could not because of the leaping flames.

She was steeling herself to make the effort anyway, when Captain Cook rushed in, shouting, "Computer, stop simulation!"

So it had been a test. Deep down, Mei-Lani had known that all along. She'd always had a special fear of fire. She had nearly died in the fire that had killed both of her parents. The captain had learned of that.

"Well, now we see what kind of officer material you are," Captain Cook said. "Your fear of fire would keep you from saving the crew."

"I'm sorry, Captain."

"Fire is always a danger. You must overcome your fears, or your fears will overcome you."

"Why are you doing this?" Mei-Lani's knees felt weak, and her voice trembled as she spoke. "I didn't think a person . . . a person like you . . . a person with your background . . . could treat other people this way." Tears came to her eyes.

"Mei-Lani, this is a very small ship." Captain Cook started to place a hand on Mei-Lani's shoulder but then didn't. "In my whole career, I've been very fortunate to be assigned to the Magnum Cruisers. They are big ships, with many people assigned to each task."

"I know. But what has that to do with me?"

"Everything!" Unexpectedly, Cook's voice sounded almost kind. "Since the *Daystar* is so small, all of us need to know each other's jobs. There is only us. We have no one else to depend on. Our lives, and the safety of the ship itself, could well depend on your ability to function in Engineering—even if there's a fire."

"Fire terrifies me!"

"I know that. But you have to overcome your fears, Mei-Lani," she repeated, "and the best way to overcome fear is to meet it head on."

Mei-Lani looked up into the captain's eyes. She knew the truth of Cook's words. "I'll try, Captain. I will really try to do my best."

"I have every confidence in you, Mei-Lani, and your best is all I can ask for. But don't be offended if I feel I have to push you—and all the Rangers." Captain Cook then extended her hand.

Mei-Lani took the captain's hand into her own and said, "Thank you, Captain."

Captain Cook stood facing the two senior officers who stood before her, Bronwen Llewellen and Zeno

Thrax. She stared at them coldly and said, "Are you presuming to tell me my duties?"

"We think that you may have taken things too far, Captain," Zeno Thrax said carefully.

"These are just young officers," the navigator said.

The captain could feel her spine stiffening. "Age does not matter. If they wear the uniform, they have to do the job."

For some time the two officers argued valiantly, but Cook cut off the argument. "I want the Rangers to be aware of their own shortcomings so that they can correct their problems. Therefore I insist on these tests!"

"But, Captain—"

"You are dismissed!"

Cook watched the two of them go out. Then she sat at her desk for a while, drumming on it with her fingers. Finally she murmured, "Why can't they understand? You've got to be tough to survive in space."

5

Battle Stations

Ringo and Raina were standing night watch on the bridge. For a long time everything had been quiet as the *Daystar* raced through space many times faster than the speed of light. Ringo was whistling a tune that Dai Bando had taught him.

Raina started humming the melody along with him. Then she said, "I remember that tune. Let me see . . . where did I hear it? And what *is* it?" Her forehead creased as she struggled to remember.

Ringo watched her rack her memory. Then he said, "Let me give you a hint."

"All right, give me a hint." She adjusted the volume control on the navigation panel.

"Deer. D-E-E-R."

"Deer? Now I'm really lost." She looked at him seriously and thought for a few moments more. "Some hint that was. Are you trying to trick me?"

"I'll give you a second hint." Ringo bent down to pick up the tuning adjuster that he had borrowed from Heck. "Heart's desire," he said as he stood up again.

"Heart's desire?" Raina placed her hands on her narrow hips. "The first hint is 'deer,' and now the second is 'heart's desire'?"

"That's right, and both are really great hints." Ringo began whistling the tune again.

Raina could hum the tune right along with Ringo's whistling, but she said, "OK, I give up. What's the name of it?"

Ringo's eyes looked up toward the ceiling as if he were searching for something. "You won't believe this," he said finally, "but I don't know the name." How could he have whistled this tune for months without knowing the name of it?

"Then just sing it," Raina ordered as she impatiently tapped her fingers on the navigation console.

"You know I can't sing. You've made fun of me enough times about that!" He always liked to please Raina, but this time was different. He had no intention of embarrassing himself in front of anyone anymore, especially her.

Dai Bando quietly walked onto the bridge just then. He must have overheard some of their conversation, because he began to sing the song. His singing voice was very good and had a soothing quality to it.

"As the deer pants for the water brooks,
So my soul pants for Thee . . ."

Raina laughed aloud. "Of course! I remember now. It's the song Dai sang for the red children. We were on the planet Ciephus on that Red Comet mission. Actually it's a verse from the Bible."

Ringo and Dai looked at each other and clapped their hands. "The young communications expert wins the prize," Ringo teased.

Raina pretended to curtsy. Then she playfully punched Ringo on the arm. "Thank you. It seems that mission happened a thousand years ago."

Ringo was too busy laughing to mind being punched. In fact, he noticed that he felt better at this moment than he had felt in most of his life before. He felt as if a great weight had been lifted off him. Something had changed. Something for the better.

Raina looked at Ringo intently. "What are you so happy about?"

"It was that song," Ringo told her. "We're to worship the Lord, and we're to trust Him, too. He's in charge. We don't need to worry about anything. That gives me a good feeling."

Dai smiled and gave Ringo a brotherly hug. "Aunt Bronwen is right again. The Lord works in mysterious ways."

Mei-Lani and Jerusha walked down the main corridor toward their quarters. Both wore their white, loose-fitting Jai Kando training outfits. Jerusha looked wilted. Mei-Lani was sure she looked the same, for Tara Jaleel had pushed them very hard today.

"I'm so glad that's over with for another day," Mei-Lani said. She was very, very tired. "I don't think I'm going to make it back to my quarters."

Jerusha had been walking silently beside her. No doubt she felt as if she had been slammed by a mad bull. Mei-Lani knew that Jerusha had positioned herself several times so that the blows that were meant for Mei-Lani wound up striking her instead.

"I've got bruises on my bruises!" Jerusha said, grinning. She flexed her shoulders and back muscles. "I'm afraid to lie down. I don't think I will be able to walk for two days."

Mei-Lani nodded her head. "I feel the same way. Well . . . maybe not quite the same way." She stopped and gently took Jerusha's arm. "Thank you for helping me. Sometimes Tara just loses it. I don't understand her. What possible enjoyment could she get out of thrashing the two of us around?"

Jerusha smiled down at her. "I've thought about Tara a lot since we were officially assigned to *Day-*

49

star." She rubbed her chin. "She said she was eager to whip us into shape. I never thought she was meaning that literally."

"I remember her saying that. It seems like yesterday. We had just completed the mission to Makon, and Sir Richard Irons attacked us. Talk about lucky. We barely escaped with our lives."

Jerusha said, "Mei-Lani, I'm ashamed of you!" she said jokingly.

"Why?"

"*Luck* had nothing to do with it. Everything happens for a reason—even the bad things. Jesus is the One we should thank for escaping with our lives. Without His help, we would've died in that crash." She gave Mei-Lani a hug. "But then, you know all that as well as I do."

"You're right, of course. And I do know better." Mei-Lani looked down. "It so easy to talk that way. I've been spending a lot of time with some of the grunts who don't know Jesus. The way they say things has rubbed off on me. It takes work to keep my mind focused on how the Lord sees things. I catch myself saying things and thinking about life the way they do."

"The Bible says that Jesus will never leave us or forsake us in our troubles. It takes work to focus on God's truth, but He wants us to."

The two girls reached Jerusha's quarters. "I'm not preaching at you, Mei-Lani," Jerusha said. "I have to remind myself of this all the time."

"You do?"

"Every single day! Especially where guys are involved." Jerusha's door opened as she toggled the door switch. "Sometimes all I seem to think about is being in love. See you later." Jerusha waved as her door closed, leaving Mei-Lani standing in the corridor.

Mei-Lani moved along and reached for the toggle switch of her own quarters. The door silently opened, and Mei-Lani slowly walked in. She felt barely able to keep her eyes open. She dropped onto her bunk and fell fast asleep.

Heck Jordan stood watching Captain Cook scan her viewer. He had been released from his cabin. The captain wanted the bridge fully manned, for the *Daystar* was fast approaching the Makon solar system.

"There is no record of this planet anywhere in Intergalactic Command files," Captain Cook said. "Thrax, reduce speed fifty percent. No sense charging in there."

Zeno Thrax was studying the data stream that ran across his console viewer. "Captain, there is something sitting on the far side of this planet. Mostly we are picking up just unclear images so far. Whatever it is, it's a *very* faint image, almost invisible. But it's *something*."

Cook looked over his shoulder. "What do you see?"

Zeno flipped through several screens, explaining each one. "See—now our normal scanners are not picking up anything, but . . ."

Cook said she saw nothing but empty space on the far side of the planet.

"But now look at this."

"My word!" Cook exclaimed, watching Zeno interconnect the scanners through the navigational array. "What are you doing? We don't have this capability on the *Cromwell*. Who designed this feature?"

The expression on the captain's face showed Heck how impressed she was. Before anyone else could utter a single syllable, he began prancing around the bridge. "It was me . . . it was me . . . it was *me*." He waved his arms about and swung his big self in a circle.

Raina and Jerusha frowned, and Raina broke into Heck's praise of himself by saying, "What a spectacle."

But Jerusha said, "Captain, Heck did design the electronic modules that made this scanning system possible. But Ringo helped him with the computer interfaces—"

"Only slightly," Heck interrupted.

Jerusha ignored him. "Raina adjusted the communications systems links, and Bronwen interfaced the computer subsystem routines with the navigational computer. So they all were involved."

"Captain, surely you are able to see who should get most of the credit," Heck said.

"But I have to admit"—Jerusha still frowned at him—"that if Heck had not invented the electronic components, none of this would have been possible."

The rest of the crew groaned.

They know that is true, Heck thought.

The captain turned back to Zeno. "Do you think that could be the Denebian starship sitting behind Makon?"

"I don't know for sure, Captain. But I can tell now that it's definitely a ship. And it definitely emits a strange radiation."

"Bring us in slowly. Maybe we can see it more clearly. At the first sign of trouble, get us out of here."

Zeno Thrax piloted the *Daystar* closer to the mystery craft. It was parked in its orbit around Makon, and it showed no sign that it knew of *Daystar*'s approach.

"Zeno, bring that ship up on the main viewer."

The first officer did so, and Jerusha gasped. "What *is* that?"

Ringo said eagerly. "I thought the design of the Amesstorites' snake ship was incredible, but this design tops that!"

Zeno Thrax began scratching his right temple thoughtfully. Then he adjusted a few more switches. "It's hard to be sure because of the radiation the craft emits. But as near as I can tell, it has the shape of a sea creature. This is either a very profound advance in ship design or . . ."

The captain watched him intently. "Or what, Zeno?" she asked.

"Captain . . . I think this ship has a cloaking device."

"Explain." Cook sat down in her chair.

"First of all, this ship exited Denebian space without so much as a peep from our deep-space beacons. Their sensors apparently didn't detect it." Zeno's face was full of puzzlement. "Second, Sir Richard Irons and his crew aboard *Jackray* may have been pirates, but they weren't stupid."

"Meaning?"

"Meaning that *Jackray's* scanners didn't pick up this ship either—that is, not until it was too late," Zeno continued. "Mostly we fly our star ships through the eyes of our computers. If the computers don't see something, then we don't see it, either. Irons never saw the ship coming. The only possible explanation is that they're using a cloaking device—a system that bends or contorts the physical characteristics of an object to sensors."

"That makes sense, Captain," the navigator added. "I don't have any idea how the Denebians are powering this device. But altering the physical signature of a ship to sensors would require tremendous power." She pointed to the viewer. "The shape of that ship reminds me of a manta ray."

"It isn't shaped like anything I've ever seen," Captain Cook said. "It's hard to identify."

Like Bronwen, Heck wondered about the source

53

of the Denebians' unusual cloaking ability, but he said nothing.

Captain Cook walked to the main viewer then, pursing her lips even tighter than normal. "Raina, use emergency encryptions and get this information to Intergalactic Command. Top priority. Heck, send along whatever schematics that you have for your scanner designs, too."

As Heck and Raina began working feverishly to complete the communications linkup, the strange ship began slowly orbiting. He realized that it was moving in *Daystar*'s direction.

"Zeno, let's back off," Captain Cook ordered. "Get us some distance from that ship."

"Aye, Captain."

The Denebian starship continued to slowly cruise around the planet in a leisurely fashion, still apparently not even aware of *Daystar*'s presence.

Captain Cook looked to be deep in thought. "Take us out seven hundred thousand kilometers," she ordered then.

"No problem, Captain. I would really like to get close to that ship, though. I would enjoy the opportunity to study everything about it. It's breathtaking."

"My hope, First, is that you don't get your opportunity today." Cook pointed at the strange craft. "We are hopelessly outgunned, outshielded, and out of our minds for being this close."

Nobody on the bridge disagreed with her.

Zeno didn't give up, however. "Captain, we could warp out of here, then swing around and come back on the far side of Makon. We'd stay low to the planet's surface and scan the Denebian ship. We'd be hard to detect. What do you think?"

Heck understood the need for Intergalactic Command to gain as much information as possible about this strange ship.

So did Captain Cook. "Go ahead, then, Mr. Thrax," she said.

The first officer engaged the Star Drive engines and headed toward open space. After two minutes, he started maneuvering in a gentle curve, coming back to Makon on the opposite side of the planet from the Denebians.

Scanners from all over the bridge began sweeping the odd-shaped ship. The *Daystar*'s computers hummed as vital data was stored in their memory.

Then, abruptly, without warning, the Denebian starship pivoted one hundred eighty degrees on its axis. Now it sped toward *Daystar*.

"Evasive, Mr. Thrax!" Cook looked over at Raina. "Send an emergency condition report to Intergalactic Command, Ensign."

Raina's hands flew over the communication console.

But it was too late. The Denebian cruiser bore down on them like an eagle attacking a rabbit. Then the rear section of the cruiser emitted a powerful green ray. It struck the *Daystar*. Heck knew the only reason they weren't vaporized instantly was that he had modified *Daystar*'s shields.

But the *Daystar* was ablaze. It plunged toward the planet's surface, engulfed in flames.

"Cook to crew!" the captain shouted into her communicator. "We are under attack. Brace for crash landing." Another green beam struck the ship. *Daystar* groaned—a sad, sad sound to Heck, who had come to love her.

"Head toward that valley, First!"

"Captain, I've lost helm control. Thrusters are offline."

The planet's surface, arid and mountainous, rushed toward them.

"Brace for impact!" Cook commanded.

The crew on the bridge held on for dear life. The *Daystar* bounced off a mountain peak. That careened it back into the atmosphere at a lower speed. The ship arced upward, then nosedived down the side of another mountain. The gentle curve of the mountain wall, descending into the valley, prevented *Daystar*'s immediately exploding in a million pieces. The ship finally came to a stop.

They were down, but now there were two worries. Even shaken as he was, Heck knew that well. Which would happen first—the *Daystar* exploding on its own or the Denebians obliterating it with another green beam?

Dazed, Ringo Smith looked about the bridge.

Captain Cook was standing with her face as white as flour. "I was the captain of the *Cromwell*, a ship with a perfect service record," she cried. "Now I've lost the *Daystar* to the Denebians!"

Bronwen Llewellen stood off to one side. She also was watching the captain. Probably she had been the only person aboard who had any sympathy for their commanding officer. But she was always tolerant of the mistakes of others. Now the navigator moved toward Captain Cook. "Captain, no one is perfect. You couldn't have known what would happen. We all make mistakes."

"I never have!" the captain murmured. "I've lost the *Daystar*. This will always be on my record."

"We can still pull out of this."

"All is lost."

Ringo Smith may have been the quietest of all the Rangers—with the possible exception of Mei-Lani Lao. But as he saw Captain Cook shaken by her failure, a sense of confidence that he had not known came over him. He could not explain it, but he suddenly believed that God had something worthwhile for him to do with his life. He certainly did not want everyone in Intergalactic Command to remember him only as the son of a space pirate.

Ringo walked over to the captain and said, "Captain, everything is going to be all right."

Captain Cook just looked at him. She still seemed dazed.

"What . . . what do you mean?"

"You're a fine captain, and now is the time for you to prove it. You've got to make some very quick decisions."

Captain Cook looked at him, seeming even more confused. She very likely was not accustomed to having support like this.

"I think you'll need to decide something right away, Captain," Ringo said. "Those Denebians are going to come looking for survivors."

The hatch door lay open, blown off its hinges, and Zeno Thrax apparently had been outside scanning the terrain. Now he returned. "Captain, there appear to be tunnel openings one hundred and eighty-five yards bearing twenty-four degrees."

Then Ivan Petroski spoke over the intercom. "Captain, we're all right in Engineering and Cargo, but the main corridor is blocked. Studs, the grunts, and myself will use the rear cargo hatch. I estimate less than ten minutes before the engines blow." Ivan's voice was full of grief.

"Do it, Engineer." The captain seemed to be more herself. "We'll head out toward the mountain from the front hatch. We'll rendezvous whenever we're safe from the Denebians."

With that, the crew members on the bridge abandoned ship and raced toward the nearest tunnel opening. They still had not reached it when the *Daystar* exploded into a fireball.

6
The Underworld

The *Daystar* bridge crew ran for their lives. The mountain looming directly in front of them made them feel like ants. At least that was Ringo's reaction. The mountain ranges that carpeted the planet Makon were enormous, he thought. They surely topped Mars's highest volcanic plateau, Olympus Mons.

"Hurry *up*, Heck!" Raina yelled, looking back at the lagging redhead. "Throw those bags away. You're going to get us all killed."

Heck was weighed down with extra gear he had grabbed up before leaving the crashed ship. He always thought ahead—at least where food and electronics were concerned, Ringo thought. Heck did drop part of his load, but not all.

The bridge crew approached the largest tunnel entrance at the base of the mountain, and Zeno started taking measurements with his datacorder. "The composition of the surface is mostly silicon," he announced. He pointed toward the cave entrance. "The silicon sparkles as it refracts the sunlight. And that may prove interesting."

"What are you talking about?" Cook asked, coming up beside him.

"I just have a hunch, that's all. It is theoretically possible that the silicon particles could refract light many miles under the planet's surface."

"Meaning what?" Cook asked impatiently. Then

apparently it dawned on her. "You mean the tunnels. The tunnels could be lit up during the day."

"Exactly. It's still a theory, but it is possible. If so, that will help us."

This tunnel entrance was manmade and centuries old, Ringo decided. It had probably been chiseled out by the inhabitants, the Dulkins, using pickaxes and shovels. An odd assortment of trees and bushes sprinkled the landscape nearby. Off in the distance was a valley of dense vegetation, and to the north of the valley lay a great forest.

Then, just before entering the tunnel, Captain Cook ordered everyone to stop and hold positions. She looked back at Jerusha. "Any sign of the Denebians?"

Jerusha waved her datacorder in several directions. "No sign of the Denebians yet, Captain," she reported.

"How about the rest of our crew?"

"It looks like they headed toward that valley over there. The readings are patchy. I think the Denebians are scanning us, and it's interrupting the readings on my datacorder." Jerusha took a few steps to the side and took another reading. "But it appears the Denebian starship is headed toward us. I estimate their arrival in five minutes."

"We've got to get out of here, and the only direction is down. Pick up your gear."

"Well, we're not overburdened with equipment, anyway," Ringo muttered. "All we have is our survival gear."

The survival gear included their envirosuits, thruster packs, Neuromags, rations, first-aid supplies, and flashlights.

"Not much to eat, either," Heck Jordan said. "I don't expect there are any fast food places down here."

"We have to move. Everybody spread out," Captain Cook ordered. "Beta formation. Dai Bando, take the lead."

"Aye, Captain." Dai replied.

The bridge crew moved into the tunnel. And Zeno Thrax was right. The silicon crystals in the tunnel walls did give off a glow that provided soft light. It was not bright lighting, but it was enough.

Ringo glanced at Mei-Lani Lao. Mei-Lani had always been frightened of underground settings. Back on Earth she had tried to go through some of the limestone caverns in Kentucky but had not been able to finish the tour. Now she peered around nervously as they walked along. "I don't like this," she said.

"It's all right," Ringo said quickly. "We'll be fine."

"I always feel like the roof of a tunnel is going to fall in on me."

Jerusha was walking beside her. "Well, this roof hasn't fallen in for hundreds of years, Mei-Lani— maybe thousands. It's not likely to fall in now."

Ringo glanced ahead at their leader, Dai Bando. Dai had said little so far. Ringo appreciated Dai. It was true that he could not operate a computer like the others, but if there came a time when they needed strength or speed, he knew that Dai would be the one they could depend on.

Zeno Thrax suddenly said, "I wonder if all the rest got out safely—Studs and Ivan and the grunts."

"They said they were using the rear escape hatch," Tara Jaleel said slowly. "I hope they did."

"I wish they were here. With us." Thrax chewed on his lower lip. His colorless eyes showed his concern. "It all happened so quickly. I just hope they got off and are safe."

Tara Jaleel then said, "So do I."

61

This surprised Ringo. The weapons officer had never shown any concern for anyone, as far as he knew.

"They're good people, Tara," Thrax said.

"Yes, they are."

"And I've failed them."

"It wasn't your fault," Jaleel said. "You had your hands full."

"Still, maybe I could have done something."

Jaleel shrugged her shoulders. "We were lucky to get out ourselves. And Jerusha's datacorder indicates that some of them made it, Zeno. Maybe they all did."

It was the first time since Ringo began serving with Tara Jaleel that he had heard her call Zeno Thrax by his given name. He stared at her. She was an officer that very few understood and almost no one liked. She was proud, aloof, and cruel at times. She was also a worshiper of the goddess Shiva, and that set her apart from most of the crew.

Jerusha said suddenly, "I've been praying all along that our friends would be all right. But I'd like to pray out loud for them. Would the rest of you mind?"

Tara Jaleel had always sneered when Christianity was mentioned, and Ringo saw Dai shoot a quick glance at her. This time, however, her face showed nothing, and she said nothing.

"I think that's a good idea," Dai said quietly.

"It's always a good idea to pray," Bronwen put in. "I've been in several spots that only God Himself could have gotten me out of."

"That's right," Ringo spoke up. "Over and over we've seen what the Lord can do. I think we ought to pray now, too. I'll do it, Jerusha." Ringo probably surprised everyone. He surprised himself. He had always been unwilling to take any responsibility. Now, however, he felt full of confidence.

Ringo prayed, "Dear Lord, we need Your help if we are to survive. Please help Ivan, and Studs, and the grunts too—wherever they are. Protect them from evil. Our trust is only in You."

"What's happened to you, Ringo?" Raina asked wonderingly, when he finished. "You're changed."

Ringo was silent for just a moment. Then he shrugged. "I don't know. Somehow, I came to the end of myself, I guess. I know I can't trust *me* and that I can always trust the Lord. They say that when you're flat on your back, there's no way to look but up."

"Does it have anything to do with the loss of your father?" she asked softly.

"In a way it does. I feel sorry for him," Ringo said. "I never really knew him, and he did wicked things, but it's always sad when anybody wastes his life."

"Yes, it is."

"I guess I was always insecure because I didn't know who my parents were," Ringo said. "And then I found out who my father was, and that made it even worse. But now I see I don't have to worry about who my father was. God just wants me to be who I am. The only thing I can say is that I'm going to trust the Lord for my future, and it feels like a great weight has been lifted from me."

Raina gave him a quick hug. "I'm proud of you, Ringo."

Ringo felt his face flush. He walked along, looking at the tunnel floor. "I don't know about that. I haven't done anything yet."

They tramped through what felt like miles of cavern. When they finally did sit down for a short rest, Captain Cook said, "I must admit I don't know where we're going. But there wasn't anywhere else to go."

"I don't know what you are thinking, Captain, but

wouldn't it be wise to try to find the Dulkin leader?" Jaleel asked. "What's his name?"

"Chief Locor," Ringo said.

Cook stared at him. "How do you know his name is Locor? It wasn't in our orders."

A silence fell over the group, and then Ringo said, "I think there are a few things you need to know about this place, Captain. Things they evidently didn't tell you in your Intergalactic Command orders."

"What sort of things?"

"It started when Captain Edge recruited us to be the crew aboard the first *Daystar*—before we actually went to work for Intergalactic Command," he began.

"Was there a first *Daystar?*" Cook's eyebrows lifted.

"That's right." Mei-Lani replied. "The *Daystar* 831."

"Our first mission was to travel to this planet and make a deal with the Dulkins for exclusive rights to a precious mineral he had found here."

"My favorite mineral," Heck said.

"Tridium," Jerusha added. "It's harder than diamonds, and since Earth is running out of diamonds, we were all going to get rich."

"That's why I signed on in the first place," Heck interrupted. "Then Commandant Lee had to show up."

"Commandant Lee?" Cook asked. "How—"

"Heck, would you be quiet?" Raina ordered. "You're confusing things." Raina continued the story herself. "Captain Edge had accidentally found Makon when he was working for Sir Richard Irons. He never told Sir Richard the location of Makon, because then Sir Richard would try to get the tridium and make himself rich. Sir Richard wanted power, and money can mean power."

"How well I know that," Cook replied.

"Anyway, after all of us almost got killed, Captain

Edge struck a deal with Chief Locor. The Dulkins would mine the tridium, and we would come back with needed supplies and educational materials for them from Intergalactic Command. Chief Locor wanted to educate his people about the galaxy."

Then Bronwen Llewellen spoke up. "Zeno and I figure that the Dulkins must have a huge amount of mined tridium stored somewhere deep inside one of these mountains. And we also believe the tridium has an energy signature that has been scanned by the Denebians."

Captain Cook studied the tunnel walls, and she frowned. "But why would a mineral like diamonds be of any interest to a people like the Denebians?" she asked.

"Because the tridium crystals have properties never dreamed of in Earth science," Heck announced matter-of-factly. "Tridium is the reason that we could scan the Denebian starship. I used tridium crystals in my electronic modules. Without tridium, our scanners would be no better than *Cromwell*'s. Tridium might even power a cloaking device."

"Are you suggesting that the Denebians might have tridium in their possession even *now?*" Captain Cook asked. She looked stunned. "Could that really be the source of energy for their cloaking device?"

"I don't know, Captain," Heck answered. "But it's curious that they have a cloaking device at all—and it's curious that they just happen to be here at the only known source of tridium in the whole galaxy."

Ringo said, "My father also found out about the crystals. His only problem was that Captain Edge wouldn't tell him where Makon was. My father was a ruthless man even at that time and would kill anyone for that knowledge. That's why he was after the *Daystar*."

Everyone sat listening, although most of them already knew the story. Captain Cook did not, of course. Her face was thoughtful all during the telling.

When Ringo finished, she said, "So your father was in some sort of conspiracy to gain control of this mineral. Maybe a conspiracy with the Denebians?"

"I think so, Captain. It might explain how he and the Denebians were both in the same area at the same time. Maybe the Denebians somehow found out about the tridium source here on Makon. Maybe they decided they didn't need my father anymore. Captain Edge didn't want my father to get control of the crystals. That would have made him too powerful. He wasn't the right man to rule over the galaxy."

Captain Cook shook her head. "I wish I had known all this earlier."

"Maybe we should have told you, Captain," the navigator said, "but we weren't sure that Intergalactic Command wanted the word spread about. Besides . . . well, with all the tests, everyone was thinking of other things . . ."

"However, I don't know if my knowing would have made any difference," Captain Cook went on thoughtfully. "We would still have been attacked, no matter what the circumstances."

"What do you think of the idea of finding the Dulkin leader, Captain?" Tara Jaleel asked.

"I can't think of anything else to do. I don't see any alternative to just continuing on and hoping to find him."

Ringo—and probably everyone else—recognized instantly that this was the second time Capt. Samantha Cook was admitting that she did not have all the answers.

"We'll all work together, and everything will be

fine, Captain," Dai Bando said quickly. "You can count on us."

Captain Cook looked around at Zeno, at Tara, and at the Rangers. An odd expression came over her face. Was she realizing how badly she had pushed them all? Yet now, everyone seemed eager to reassure her. She flushed and then said, "I . . . I'm grateful for your cooperation."

"Why, of course, Captain." Dai Bando smiled. "And we'll come out of this all right. The Lord won't let us down."

7

Two Tunnels

The bridge crew plodded along the dimly lit tunnel. The ground ahead sloped downward gently but steadily. There was something frightening about the whole thing, not only to Mei-Lani, who didn't like tunnels, but also to the rest of the group. Even Zeno Thrax felt it, and he was used to underground living. Captain Cook herself was now in advance, holding one of the emergency torches to provide more light.

Behind him, Dai Bando murmured to Jerusha, "Have you noticed the sides of the tunnel?" The boy's voice sounded tense, which was unusual for Dai.

"Only that they're glittering, and the glitter gives off some light. What about them?"

"The glitter makes me think they've got some kind of metal in them."

"Well, that's natural enough. Maybe it's just the silicon crystals."

Dai Bando said no more, and for a while the only sound was the tramp of their marching feet.

Just then a warm breeze filled the passage, and Zeno said, "Feel that? There must be air holes somewhere. We're getting deep enough where breathing might be a problem, otherwise."

"I don't see any light coming down through air holes," Tara Jaleel said.

"No, I don't either. You know," he said then, "this is a lot like my home planet."

Jaleel turned her head to stare at him. "I never

understood how anybody could live underground like worms."

"It's not so bad when you are used to it."

"I don't think I'd want to get used to it. It sounds terrible. I'll take the sunlight anytime."

Zeno did not argue, but as he tramped along with the others, his mind went back to when he had lived on his native planet. Everyone there lived underground, for no life could survive on the surface. Loneliness came over him. He had never gotten used to being an alien.

Down, down, down they went, using a couple of flashlights now to brighten the tunnel. Then they paused once again to rest and to drink sparingly from their canteens.

"Better be careful with the water supply," Captain Cook warned. "We don't know when we'll find something else to drink."

But Heck said, "I thought most caves had springs or underground rivers or something like that."

"That may be, but we don't know that is true here."

"And I'm getting hungry too," he said. "Can't we have a little bit to eat now?"

"Better hold off on that, Jordan. I know you're hungry, but you may be hungrier later."

"And I don't think it's likely that we'll find much to eat down here," Mei-Lani said.

"Well, the Dulkins live down here someplace, don't they? So they've found something to eat," Heck argued. "Maybe they learned to raise vegetables on the surface or something like that."

"Time to move on," Captain Cook said.

They went on down the tunnel.

Heck was growing weary. Besides, he worried

about something else. "What will we do when all our flashlights burn out?" he asked with a frown.

"We'd have to get along with just the light from the walls—like we did at the beginning," Raina said. "But I think we'll find something before then. The Dulkins are bound to be down here somewhere."

But if the Dulkins were there, there was little sign of them. All kept watching for some indication of the presence of people, but they found none.

And then they came to a fork in the tunnel. The main passage went straight on, but another bore off to the right. The righthand tunnel was also headed downhill, but it was smaller.

"It looks like we've got to make a decision," Zeno said.

"You're right, Thrax, and it's a hard one."

"I think we ought to stay on the main tunnel, Captain," Tara Jaleel said. "It's more likely to lead to where we want to go. The other one is smaller . . ."

"Still, the side tunnel may be the one we ought to take." Captain Cook looked thoughtful. "Where does it lead? Let's take a break here and have a bite to eat. And think."

It was a welcome break. They all settled themselves down and began to eat hungrily. Heck and Ringo sat together, leaning against the tunnel wall.

Heck was about to eat all of his food supply, but Ringo stopped him. "You'll starve to death later if you don't save some of it."

"But what I ate wasn't enough to even make a dent in me."

"I know it wasn't much, but we've got to be careful, Heck. We still don't know where we're going. Or how long we'll be down here."

Heck looked around and chewed his lower lip. "I

71

never did like being underground. I agree with Mei-Lani on that."

"We'll be all right. You wait and see. The Lord won't forsake us."

"I'm not a Christian," Heck heard himself say.

Ringo quickly looked at him. "This might be a good time for you to consider that, Heck."

There was something ominous about being so far underground, Heck thought. This tunnel was too much like a grave with the ends kicked out. But Heck's stubbornness welled up, and he shook his head. "Naw, I can take care of myself. I'll do all right. Plenty of time for God when I get older—and richer!"

"You may not get older. You can't know when your turn to die will come. And we're in a dangerous spot."

"Nothing's going to get me," Heck said. He got up and went over to sit beside Dai Bando.

However, that turned out to be not much better, for Dai had overheard the conversation with Ringo.

"I think you should listen to what Ringo said," Dai told him. "You need Jesus. All of us do." He spoke with a gentle tone. "No one knows the exact time they will die, Heck—including you. Any day could be your last day. You have to be prepared so that you'll be ready, no matter what."

Actually Heck had been very impressed by the faith—and the lives—of the other Space Rangers. As a matter of fact, he sometimes felt left out and lonely and wished that he had committed himself to Jesus a long time ago. But he had always been afraid that God would ask him to do something hard. Heck loved money and things. He was determined to be rich. And from what he had heard, he was fairly certain that Christians were not to focus on getting wealthy.

Almost angrily Heck said, "I'm tired of listening to

you guys! I *will* get the tridium, and I *will* be rich—you'll see!" He got up again and went off to sit by himself this time, his head down.

Sitting on the other side of Dai, Jerusha had been listening. "It's too bad," she said sadly.

"Yes, it is. Heck's kind of obnoxious on the outside, but down deep inside he's just like the rest of us. He needs Jesus."

"Just like everybody does. But he's so *stubborn*."

And then Captain Cook stood up. She said, "Well, I've come to a decision."

"So which tunnel shall we take, Captain?" Tara Jaleel asked.

"I'm going to split the group. Dai Bando—you, Tara, Jerusha, Raina, and Bronwen, you'll be in one group. I'll take the others with me—Zeno, Ringo, Mei-Lani, and Heck."

"I think you're making a mistake, Captain," Tara said boldly.

Captain Cook looked into the angry eyes of the weapons officer and said, "Dai Bando will lead the second group."

"Dai Bando!" Tara Jaleel cried with indignation. "Why, Bando can't lead anything!"

"He is my choice, Lieutenant Jaleel, and you'll be under his orders."

Jerusha glanced at Jaleel's face. The weapons officer was furious. It was clear that she felt she was being put down, and she could not bear that. Probably she wanted to strike out at Captain Cook but knew that was impossible. Jaleel clamped her lips together and said nothing more.

"We've got to concentrate on finding Chief Locor,"

Captain Cook said. "This will give us a better opportunity to locate some Dulkins."

Jerusha spoke up. "From the reports I've heard from Captain Edge, Captain, the chief actually is a very fine person. I'm sure he'll help us."

"If we can find him!" Tara Jaleel muttered.

"We'll have to find him. We don't have any way to radio back to Intergalactic Command," Cook said, "and our only hope for survival is to get help from somewhere."

"What is likely to happen, Captain Cook?" Mei-Lani asked timidly.

"Sooner or later, when home base recognizes that contact's been lost, they'll send somebody looking for us. If we could radio, then help would get here sooner. But in the meantime, we've got to stay out of the way of the Denebians."

"You're right about that, Captain. Those Denebians are a bad bunch," Thrax said.

Captain Cook stood still for a moment more. "Again, tell me what makes this tridium so valuable anyway?"

Heck set in again to explain the power of the crystals. "Like I told you, Captain, whoever has these crystals will become the most powerful person in the galaxy. They focus energy. If I took a tridium crystal the size of grain of sand and focused a Neuromag beam through it, I could aim at this mountain, and the mountain would turn to dust."

Captain Cook frowned. "Those crystals sound like highly potent material. I can see why it wouldn't do for them to fall into the wrong hands."

"That's right, Captain," Zeno Thrax said. "And I think that's exactly why Intergalactic Command sent us on this mission. We can't fail. If the Denebians get their hands on tridium, you know what will happen."

"It wouldn't be pleasant," Captain Cook said. "All right. We'll separate here. Bando, take the main tunnel. The first group to find the Dulkin leader will come back and trace the steps of the other."

"I still don't like it," Tara Jaleel muttered. "We ought to stay together."

Captain Cook stared at the weapons officer and shook her head. "Our chances are better this way. Now, let's get on with it."

8

The Captives

Captain Cook led her group on down the steep, right-hand passageway. It appeared to be descending into the very bowels of the planet. She did not talk, for she was troubled. Ordinarily she never questioned her own orders, but this was like nothing she had ever experienced. As they went down ever deeper, she began to wonder if she should have divided the group. Yet her captain's instincts told her to stand firm.

Zeno Thrax marched along slightly behind the captain. He knew she was disturbed, and he kept close watch on her. Being underground did not bother Zeno as much as it did the others, but he could tell that his companions were not happy. He glanced back and saw Ringo, Mei-Lani, and Heck bringing up the rear. He wondered how they would perform if they ran into trouble. *They've proven themselves in the past*, he thought, *but they're young, and you never know.*

"Are you all right, Mei-Lani?" Ringo asked. He slowed down and took her arm. He thought he knew how she felt. Her eyes were large and frightened. "The tunnels reflect the light from our torches in eerie ways, don't they? But they give off light, and that's good."

"I'm all right," Mei-Lani answered. But she obviously was feeling very insecure.

"It's a bad scene, but we'll get out of it."

Heck Jordan came up beside them then and kept

pace. He too acted nervous about being in the partial darkness. He said, "I don't like any of this. I think we should have stayed up on the surface."

"Those Denebians would have found us right off, Heck. You know that."

"Well, maybe they're not as bad as everybody thinks."

"I think they're probably worse," Ringo said. "At least from all reports I've heard."

The three trudged on at the end of the line.

"I guess I don't mind admitting it—" Mei-Lani said. "I'm truly scared."

"None of us like it down here," Ringo said. "But we know the Lord is with us. And He has a good plan for us. Remember? You always keep saying that."

Ahead of them, he saw Zeno Thrax look back over his shoulder. "I'd better hurry them along, Captain," Zeno said. "They're falling behind."

"All right, Thrax, see to it."

Zeno stood and waited until the three stragglers caught up with him. "You're falling too far behind," he said.

"What difference does it make, Zeno?" Heck said. "This tunnel's not going anywhere, anyhow."

"It leads somewhere," Thrax answered. "Anyway, we don't want to fall behind. Move along now. I'll drop back and bring up the rear myself."

"Zeno's right," Ringo said. "Let's keep moving." He kept his tight hold on Mei-Lani's hand, and he could tell that comforted her.

Captain Cook marched down the tunnel without slackening her pace. She had begun to notice that the passage was growing broader. Now there were several side entrances, and that encouraged her. "Maybe we'll find our way out of this place yet. I would certainly like to see daylight."

She had not gone more than ten paces after muttering this when she suddenly stopped dead still, and her heart leaped in her breast.

Ahead of her loomed a monstrous beast. The creature reminded her of a gorilla but was even more fierce-looking. It had fangs and red eyes and a powerful body with sharp talons on all four limbs.

Captain Cook had faced some dangerous situations in her career, but she had never faced anything like this. She tugged at her Neuromag. But before she could get it out of its holster the beast was upon her.

She struggled and cried out, trying to keep away from the animal's teeth, fighting back with all her might.

She was dimly aware that the others had run forward.

"What is it?" Mei-Lani was screaming.

Then Ringo Smith was there with his Neuromag. Without a moment's hesitation he placed the barrel of the weapon against the beast's head and fired. The creature let out a scream, then fell to one side.

Captain Cook was not sure at first what had happened. She had been prepared for death, and even now the weight of the beast was on her. She pushed at it, then felt the animal's body being dragged away. Someone was saying, "Are you all right, Captain?"

A hand pulled her to her feet, and she looked into the face of Ringo Smith.

"Are you all right, Captain?" he asked again.

"I'm all right, Smith."

"Good. That was an awful thing."

All stood looking down at the slain beast.

"I wouldn't want to meet a creature like that without a Neuromag," Thrax said. "I'm sorry, Captain. I should have been here to help you."

"You were doing your duty, First." Captain Cook turned to Ringo then. "Thank you, Smith," she said warmly. "You saved my life."

"Well, I'm glad it turned out all right."

"This thing smells!" Heck exclaimed. He poked at the animal with his toe, and then a thought seemed to come to him. "Hey, if there's one of these, there may be others down here!"

"That's right," Thrax said. "Everyone set your Neuromags on kill." Then he stared with admiration at Ringo. "You really moved fast, Ensign. I didn't know you had it in you."

"I'm glad he did," Captain Cook said.

The captain and the others patted Ringo on the back and bragged on him so much that his face flushed. "I guess we'd better get going," he said.

"We sure don't want to meet a herd of these," Heck said.

"Come along," Captain Cook said. "We'll come to the end of this tunnel sooner or later and find what's there." She started on down the passage, leaving the dead monster behind. But she did take time to say, "No one ever saved my life before, Ringo. I owe you a special debt."

Ringo smiled. "It's all right, Captain. I'm glad I was here."

Dai Bando and his squad progressed slowly down the main tunnel. The passage was narrower now, but Dai still felt hopeful.

Tara Jaleel, however, had been complaining ever since the two parties separated. "We may as well go back," she said, now sounding totally disgusted.

"The captain's orders were to go on," Dai told her. "We have to obey."

"Hey, what's this?" Jerusha was bending over and picking up an object. "It looks like a kind of shoe."

Everyone crowded around, and Dai turned his light on the object in her hand. "It *is* a shoe. It looks like a child's shoe."

"Well, the Dulkins are very small people—like dwarfs. Like children," Raina said. "They are shorter than Mei-Lani."

Bronwen said, "This is encouraging. At least finally we know we're on the right track."

"Let's double-time it," Dai cried excitedly. He started off at a dead run but soon heard a faint cry from behind him. He looked back and saw that he had completely outdistanced the others. There was no way they could keep up with his superior speed. "That's no way to act," he told himself, and he ran back. "Sorry. I just got carried away."

"I wish we all could run as fast as you can, Dai," Raina said with admiration.

"He has always been the fastest thing on two feet." Bronwen smiled. "I've always been proud of my nephew's speed."

"Well, speed won't help us if we meet up with some of those Denebians—except to run away!" Tara Jaleel grumbled.

Dai knew the weapons officer was still disgruntled that she had not been appointed leader. She was going to find fault every way she could think of.

"Let's go on," Dai said. "We must be getting close to something if we're starting to find garments. At least we know people have been here."

They moved forward, everyone looking closely for other signs of life.

"I wish we'd find some food, that's what I wish. A can of beans, even," Heck whined.

Bronwen smiled. "I doubt if we'll find canned food down here."

On they went, and then Dai Bando stopped abruptly. "Wait one minute," he whispered.

"What is it, Dai?" Jerusha asked quickly, keeping her voice down.

"I hear something up ahead."

"What does it sound like? I don't hear a thing."

"It sounds like voices."

"*I* don't hear anything," Tara Jaleel said. "It's nothing!"

"Dai's ears are very good. I think we'd better assume someone's up there."

"I'll tell you what," Dai said thoughtfully. "Why don't the rest of you stay here for a time, and let me sneak up on them."

"I'm the weapons officer! I should go with you."

"All right, Lieutenant Jaleel. The two of us, then. The rest of you stay right here."

Dai moved forward with Tara Jaleel at his side. "We'd better turn off these lights and just use the glow that comes from the walls. Whoever's up there could see us coming," he said.

Tara Jaleel turned off her torch, following Dai Bando's example, and they crept forward. Soon the sound of voices became louder.

They rounded a turn, and Dai put out a hand and touched Tara Jaleel's arm. "There they are," he whispered.

"I see them. I could get them from here."

Tara Jaleel was raising her Neuromag.

Shocked, Dai shoved her arm upward. "You can't kill them!"

"We don't know who they are."

"Right. We don't even know that they're enemies. They look harmless enough."

Dai had extraordinary eyes. Both his sense of sight and sense of hearing were extremely well developed.

"What do they look like?" Jaleel asked, squinting down the passage.

"There are two of them, and they look like dwarfs to me. They're thick and short, and no taller than Ivan. Let's sneak up on them. I'll grab one, and you grab the other. But don't hurt them."

They inched along, and the voices of the dwarfs became more distinct. Now Dai could hear that they were speaking the common intergalactic dialect.

One dwarf was saying, "We need to get back to the rest of the tribe. We've been gone too long."

"We know that someone has invaded the tunnels. We must carry a report back. We have plenty of time."

"We can't carry a report back if they kill us."

"Oh, Blib, you're always looking on the dark side of things."

"Well, let me tell you, Spiny, if you'd listen to me, you'd know a lot more."

The two were bickering so loudly that they did not hear the two silent figures that came upon them. The first thing they seemed to know was the feel of arms going around them.

"They've got me, Spiny!" one yelled. "Run!"

"No one's running anywhere," Tara Jaleel said. She was holding one of the figures with ease, although he was kicking and screaming.

Dai held the other dwarf with one hand. Then he turned on his light to see more clearly what they had captured. The two men were very short but had large, muscular legs. This was due, Dai knew, to the heavy gravity on Dulkin. They were cave dwellers so were very pale. Both wore odd-looking fur hats, and their coarse hair hung down over their foreheads. Both of them wore clothing that looked like patchwork quilts sewn into shirts and trousers.

"Who are you?" Dai asked gently.

"Who are *you?*" the one called Spiny demanded. "Put me down!"

"In a moment. We need to identify you."

Spiny said, "Don't tell them anything, Blip. They've come to steal from us."

"We haven't come to steal anything," Dai Bando said. "Our ship was wrecked on the surface."

"We know. We heard it, and we saw it. And we saw you leave the wreckage, too," Spiny said.

"Yes," Blip added, "and we're going back to tell our chief."

"Is his name Locor?" Dai Bando asked quickly.

The two Dulkins looked at him. "How did you know that?"

"We're friends of Capt. Mark Edge—who is a friend of Chief Locor."

"Captain Edge. He was here once. He was a nice man," Blip said.

"What do you want with us?" Spiny was still suspicious.

"We're looking for Chief Locor. We need his help."

"Chief Locor won't be happy to see you," Spiny promised, looking sullen. "Every time somebody comes in a spaceship, we have trouble. Why don't you just leave?"

"We don't have any way to leave," Dai said. "Remember? Our cruiser is wrecked. You're going to have trouble all right, but not from us. There are some really bad people headed your way."

"What people?"

"The Denebians."

Fear showed instantly on the faces of the two Dulkins.

"Not them!" Spiny moaned. "Anybody but them."

"They're coming, and that's why we need to talk to Chief Locor. Can you take us to him?"

The two Dulkins were silent for a while, but finally Blip said, "We'll have to do it, Spiny. We'll take them to the chief, and he'll decide what to do."

"All right. Come with us. We have a long way to go."

9
Underground Sailors

W hat's that up ahead?"
Ringo Smith had been walking alongside
Captain Cook when he suddenly saw something glimmering in the dim light ahead. At first he was unsure, but then he knew that *something* was there. "It looks like water!" he cried.

Instantly everyone in the bridge group grew excited. All had become weary of this endless tunnel.

"It is!" Heck shouted. "Boy, I hope it's good to drink!"

"It probably is. I don't see how water could be polluted way down here," Mei-Lani said. "Come on. I'm so thirsty."

"Not so fast," Captain Cook warned. "We'd better be careful. We don't know what's up there besides water."

"The captain's right," Zeno Thrax warned. "Be on the alert. We don't want to meet any enemies down here—not as few as we are."

"Ah, we haven't seen a soul. And for sure nobody's going to find us down here," Heck said. "I'm thirsty."

"We can go forward but very slowly." Captain Cook, with those words, began to advance cautiously. "The tunnel floor is almost level now, have you noticed? That body of water is almost surely some kind of a lake."

And suddenly they were out of the passage and in an enormous cavern.

Here, something—apparently more silicon crystals in the walls, Ringo guessed—lit up the cave. The cavern ceiling rose as far as he could see.

Captain Cook looked around in all directions. "I still can't understand the lighting in this place."

"It's the crystals in the walls," Heck said. "They glow like some kind of old fluorescent lighting."

"Whatever it is, I'm thankful for it," Ringo said. "I'm tired of gloomy tunnels."

The water was a dark blue-green, almost as murky as the North Atlantic back on Earth.

Heck looked on impatiently as Zeno examined his datacorder.

"There is a variety of aquatic life in this body of water," the first officer announced. "And the bottom is deeper than the range of this scanner."

"That would make it over fifty miles deep!" Heck exclaimed.

"At the very least, Ensign," Zeno replied. "At the very least." He stooped over the edge and tested the water. "And, Captain," he said, looking at the datacorder's reading, "this water is remarkably clean. It's safe to drink."

"That's good news," Captain Cook said. "Go ahead and drink, and be sure you all fill your canteens."

Heck Jordan and the other young members of the crew threw themselves face down at the water's edge.

"I wouldn't care if it's poison. I've got to have a drink," Heck said defiantly. He lowered his face and scooped up a handful. "It's good!" he bubbled. "It's real good." The water seemed to soak into his thirsty tissues.

Beside him, Mei-Lani drank long and deep. "This is such good water," she murmured.

When Zeno and the captain had slaked their thirst and all had filled their canteens, they began to look around more carefully.

"I don't see any signs of anybody, but somehow I feel that a lake in a cavern this big wouldn't go unnoticed," Captain Cook murmured.

"I'll bet you're right, Captain," Ringo said eagerly. "We're bound to run into some Dulkins soon."

"I hope so," Mei-Lani said. "That trip through the tunnel was the loneliest thing I ever went through. I don't want to go back."

"Well, we've learned one thing about the Dulkins," Zeno said.

"What's that, Thrax?" the captain asked.

"Now we know what they eat. This is fresh water—with fish in it. I've even seen one or two break the water. And if there's fresh water, the Dulkins could grow some sort of mushrooms down here. Another thing, if there's fresh water below the surface, there's almost certain to be fresh water above. So they may have some sort of gardens that would get a little sunlight."

Heck listened to the two of them talk. He couldn't help noticing that Captain Cook was much more humble than she had been when she had first stepped on board the *Daystar*.

Then he heard the first officer say, unexpectedly, "The Rangers do well, don't they, Captain?"

There was a moment's silence, and then the captain nodded. "Much better than I had dreamed they would. I believe I was wrong about them, First."

"You can't be totally blamed for that, Captain. Age can be deceptive. They look so young. And we always expect excellence to go along with age."

"I've learned a lesson, though, and I'm glad for it."

They all sat by the underground lake, resting and glad to have brighter light once more.

Then the captain said, "Let's start skirting the lake. Time may be running out. We've got to find the Dulkins—and their leader. I hope Chief Locor will listen to reason."

"I feel sure he will," Zeno said. "Captain Edge always said he's a very reasonable man. He had a lot of regard for Chief Locor."

"Well, that's encouraging. Let's see what we can find."

It would take some time to circle the lake. They walked slowly, at the same time also looking for other tunnels that might lead out from the cavern.

And then Ringo, who had gone on ahead, called back excitedly in a voice that echoed, "Come and see what I found!"

"What is it, Smith?" the captain cried eagerly. She and the others rushed forward to see.

He pointed proudly.

"A boat!"

"A boat, Captain," Ringo said. "And see—there are even some oars here."

"So now we know for sure that we're on the right track," Captain Cook said. "What I think we'll do," she announced after a moment, "is save some time by crossing straight over to the other side."

"I think we'll have to, anyway, Captain," Ringo said. "Look ahead. Pretty soon, we can't go any farther along the shore. The shoreline is blocked off with those huge rocks. We'll have to cross this underground sea if we're going to get anywhere."

Captain Cook and First Officer Thrax examined the boat.

"Not in very good shape, Zeno."

"It's not. We may have to patch it up a little."

"We don't have much to patch with, but let's see what we can do."

It was a good-sized boat, too—close to twenty feet long with a broad beam of almost five feet. The crew put it in the water and tested it by all climbing into it. Actually, the craft turned out to be in better shape than either of the officers had first thought.

Finally Captain Cook said, "All right. We'll do it. We'll take turns with the oars. Shove off, Thrax."

Thrax grinned at her. "This is going back into history, isn't it, Captain?"

For the first time since Ringo had met Captain Cook, he saw her smile broadly. "It's not exactly the *Daystar*. Instead of Mark V Star Drives, we've got four paddles. But we'll use what we have."

"Yes, we will, Captain," Zeno said. "Let me take that oar."

The captain herself took one oar and the first officer another. Ringo and Heck took the final two. Mei-Lani, Ringo thought, would not have been much use anyway, small as she was. She sat on one of the seats and kept careful watch.

The boat was slow, for it had a square front and did not cleave the water very well. The four rowers worked hard.

Ringo was not surprised that it was Heck who complained first. "This is a terrible way to get from one place to another. I think we should use the thruster packs."

"No, we have to reserve the thrusters for a real emergency," Cook said.

"This is better than swimming," Ringo panted. "We're making progress, anyway."

"I'm just so glad for better light," Mei-Lani said. "It was awful going through that gloomy tunnel."

"Darkness—even semidarkness—can be rather frightening," Captain Cook said. "I don't like it myself. And I still don't understand where this light is coming from."

"Some kind of mineral—like Zeno says," Ringo said.

They paddled on until they grew tired. They took a short rest and then continued.

"I see something!" Mei-Lani called out suddenly.

"What?" Ringo asked.

"Something in the water over there. Some kind of a fish."

"I don't see anything," Heck said, squinting in the artificial light.

"But there was something. I saw it. There—you can see the ripples."

Indeed there were broad ripples in the area where Mei-Lani was pointing.

"Just a fish, I expect," Zeno said. "We may have to come back later and try to catch some. If we can figure out how to cook it."

"I wouldn't mind that," Ringo said. "I always liked to fish."

"No telling whether they'd be good to eat on this planet or not."

"Any kind of fish is good to eat," Heck said, smacking his lips. "Nothing like fried fish."

Mei-Lani laughed. "You'd eat anything, Heck."

They paddled on. For a while the only sound in the cavern was the splashing of the oars. And then Captain Cook cried out, "There's the shore ahead! One more drive now, and we'll be there."

With a final effort that exhausted him, Ringo felt the prow of the boat grind on the beach.

Immediately the captain dropped her oar and jumped out. "Help me, Zeno!"

Zeno leaped out and held the boat steady while the others climbed out.

"We'd better pull this boat well up on shore to be sure it's safe. We may have to use it in case we need to retrace our steps," Captain Cook said.

"That's a good idea, Captain," Zeno said.

They pulled the boat fully onto shore and turned it upside down over the oars. Only then did they look around.

"Hard to tell much about this place," Zeno said.

"Let's start out this way," Captain Cook said. "We're likely to find a tunnel entrance."

Ringo and the others trudged along after the captain. By now Ringo was not only tired but hungry. He guessed the rest felt the same. They said little. Not even Heck.

"It's been a long day's march, Mei-Lani," Ringo said. "I wish we could take a rest. I know you're tired."

Indeed, Mei-Lani looked extremely tired, but she was not one to complain. "I'm all right," she said. "I just want to find the Dulkins."

On and on they went along the shoreline. There were no tunnel entrances. It was discouraging. But at last the captain said, "Finally! I see something up there on the beach."

"What is it?" Heck asked. "Food?"

They all began running, but then Captain Cook stopped. "Oh no!" she cried.

"What is it, Captain?" Ringo asked.

"It's the boat! We've come in a circle. This is not the other side of the lake. It's an island we're on."

"An island!" Mei-Lani cried. "What a disappointment!"

The captain stood thinking. "What we'll have to do is row around this island and then on to the other side of the lake." She looked at Mei-Lani and quickly said, "But not now. I know you're all tired. So, first, we're going to take a nap."

Soon everyone was lying down, using their packs for pillows.

Heck was as tired as the rest and even hungrier. No one had said anything about eating, and the thought came to him of going fishing. But he was too worn out for that.

He did drop off to sleep and, being a sound sleeper, slept hard for a time. When he woke up, he saw that the others were still lying motionless.

Heck got to his feet. He thought, *It's plain to see that I'm the toughest one here.* Then he grinned and murmured, "I'll just take a look around this island."

Ringo came awake, startled by a sound. He saw Captain Cook jump to her feet and draw her Neuromag.

"I heard it, too, Captain," Zeno Thrax said. Now he too was up and had his weapon drawn.

Mei-Lani and Ringo came to their feet, Mei-Lani asking, "What is it?"

"I don't know. It sounded like somebody shouting," Thrax said, puzzled.

Then Ringo said with surprise in his voice. "Listen to that."

"We *are* listening. Who do you think it is?" Mei-Lani asked.

"I think it's Heck yelling," Ringo said. "See? He's the only one not here, and it sure sounds like him."

"It's Heck all right," Thrax said after listening a moment more. "Well, come on. He's probably in trouble. That or he's found something to eat."

The four of them hurried toward the yelling, and before long they came upon Heck Jordan.

"What are you hollering about, Heck?" Ringo called to him.

Heck seemed in the mood to turn cartwheels. "I found it!" he shouted. "I found it!"

The others closed in curiously. Heck was pointing to a hole in the cave floor. "Just look in there."

As they all crowded around, Captain Cook asked, "But what *is* it?"

"It's *tridium* crystals. That's what it is. Somebody mined them and buried them in this hole. There was this suspicious-looking pile of rocks, so I moved them, and it's *tridium*, and it's worth its weight in diamonds! We're all billionaires! Hooray!"

Ringo picked up a crystal and examined it. He had heard much about tridium, and now here it was, the actual thing. But he put it back, saying, "We're not out of here yet."

"No, but we know where this is," Heck said excitedly. "All we've got to do is come back, take one load, and we can do anything that we want the rest of our lives."

The captain too examined the crystals. Then she said, "Well, this is all very fine, but we can't take them with us now. And we certainly don't want the Denebians to find them—or take them from us."

"What'll we do, then, Captain?" Thrax questioned.

"First of all, we'll cover up the tridium. Then we'll go back to the boat. We'll circle the island, and we'll row to the other side of this lake. We've got to find the Dulkins soon. I've got a bad feeling that something very unpleasant is getting ready to happen."

They trudged back to the boat, loaded their gear, and prepared to shove off.

Suddenly Mei-Lani said, "Has anybody else noticed that there are a lot more fish stirring now?"

Ringo looked, and indeed the water was astir. Everywhere he looked, it seemed, there were swirling circles where something had broken the surface. "It's full of fish all right," he muttered. "And some of them may not be good for our health."

"You mean piranha or something like that?" Heck asked. His hand had been dangling in the water, and he quickly drew it out.

"We don't know what kind of fish they are," the captain said grimly. "And the quicker we get away from this lake, the better I'll feel about it. Get ready to row fast."

10
The Attack

How much farther is it?" Dai Bando asked. Although he and Tara Jaleel were still fresh, he saw that Raina and Bronwen and even Jerusha were exhausted.

"Not far," the dwarf Blib said. "Almost there."

"It's far," Spiny said.

The trip had taken much longer than Dai had imagined it would. Raina was not an athletic type, and she was clearly worn out. Bronwen's older age was ordinarily not a problem, but now her breath was coming in gasps.

"We've got to slow down, Dai," Jerusha said.

"I see that. Look, why don't the three of you wait here? Tara and I will go on and see what's up ahead."

"No, just give us a little break, and we can all go," Bronwen panted. "I don't want us to be separated."

Tara Jaleel was impatient. "I think Dai's right. The two of us need to go on by ourselves."

The two Dulkins took no part in this conversation. They had been acting rather uneasy around these aliens to their planet, and they just stood waiting. They themselves seemed to be tireless. They had clumped along on their stubby legs and talked to each other but hardly at all to the others.

Blib said, "It is only a mile from here. Perhaps less."

Spiny said, "It's more than that."

"No. A mile and maybe not that far."

Dai had learned that the two rarely agreed on anything. Finally he made the decision. "We'll rest here for a while. Everybody take a break."

Jerusha, Raina, and Bronwen Llewellen at once took off their packs and lay down to rest. All three appeared to go to sleep at once.

Tara Jaleel paced about, while the two Dulkins sat whispering to each other. Dai sat, but his eyes were alert. Though he himself was practically tireless, he was concerned about the welfare of the weaker members of the crew.

"What do you think we'll find ahead, Lieutenant Jaleel?" he asked when she too sat down.

"The Dulkins. What else?"

"I'm a little concerned about the Denebians," Dai said. "You know more about them than I do. Aren't they quite advanced?"

Tara Jaleel nodded. "They have some awesome weapons."

"So these Dulkins wouldn't have much chance against them in battle, would they?"

"No chance whatsoever. The *Daystar* could have fought them off with our technology, if they hadn't taken us by surprise. But it's too late to talk about that."

He sat silent for a while, his eyes searching the tunnel ahead. "It'll be all right," he said at last. "What happens may be difficult, but the Lord will see to it that it's all right."

Tara Jaleel snorted. Perhaps she was more fatigued than she wanted to admit or was still irritated by the fact that the captain had chosen Dai to be the leader. "You always say things will be all right. 'The Lord will make it all right.' Well, things are not always all right. Don't you know that? Are you entirely stupid?"

"I know God permits bad things to happen some-times."

"Then why don't you act like it? What'll probably happen is that we'll get blasted out of existence by those Denebians."

"I just believe God knows what He is doing. He'll do for us what He sees is best. He always does."

"I don't know why anyone would think that!"

"Because He says so in His Book." Dai knew the odds were against them. But there was truly no fear in him, because he also knew that God was in control of everything that happened.

"Don't you ever get lonely, lieutenant?" he asked suddenly.

Jaleel shot him an indignant glance. "What are you talking about?"

"You're always by yourself. You never have anything to do with the rest of the crew. Do you have family?"

The question seemed to trouble Lieutenant Jaleel. Perhaps she had no family. She certainly had no friends. She was a fiercely independent woman. She said quickly, "I don't need anybody."

"We all need somebody. I certainly do," Dai Bando said. "The Lord Himself wants to be your friend. I'd like to be your friend, too. I have always wanted that."

The hard face of Lieutenant Jaleel melted, and in place of the hardness there was a hungry expression. Dai sensed that, for one moment, something had changed.

"We all need friends," he repeated. "There's a verse in the Bible that says two are better than one."

"I don't believe that—or anything else in your Bible."

"I'm sure you believe some of the Bible," Dai said. "The Bible says that we're all going to die."

"I don't need the Bible to believe that." Tara Jaleel snorted again. "And I don't need God, and if I did, I wouldn't have a weak God like yours."

"Why would you call Him a weak God?"

"He died, didn't He? He was nailed to a cross."

"That's what He came for, Lieutenant Jaleel. He came to die in our place for our sins, and He did."

"A strong God wouldn't allow Himself to die."

"Lieutenant, did you ever see a strong crew member give his life for another? Was that a sign of weakness?"

He was sure that Tara Jaleel had seen this happen more than once.

But she sat silent, her face turned away from him. "That's neither here nor there," she said at last, but her voice sounded very uncertain.

"I think it's important, Lieutenant." Dai spoke softly, and he did not seem to be arguing so much as talking to himself. "Jesus came for one reason. To die for the sins of the world—for sinners like me."

"How can one die for another in that way? It doesn't make any sense."

"It doesn't make sense in the same way that two plus two equals four. But it's so."

"How can you know that?"

"Again, because His Book, the Bible, says so. From the moment I asked God to forgive my sins because of the shed blood of Jesus, things changed for me. That's always true. Haven't you noticed that there's something different about Christians?"

"You Christians are just living in a fool's paradise. When we die, we're dead. And that's it."

"And I don't think you believe that, Lieutenant."

Jaleel turned to face him, the one person she had never been able to defeat physically. Time and again in their practice bouts she had slashed at him, obviously trying to kill him with one blow. Dai knew that. But God had helped him to simply duck under her blows. He could have ruined her with his tremendous strength, but he never did. And she knew that. Nor did he ever allow himself to show anger when she cursed and insulted him.

"Never mind what I believe. Let's just get out of here. You think they've rested long enough?"

"Give them another half hour."

The half hour passed slowly for those who waited. Then, reluctantly, Dai went over and spoke to the sleepers. "I think we'd better move on."

All struggled back to consciousness and got to their feet.

"I feel better now, nephew," Bronwen said.

"And I feel *much* better," Mei-Lani chimed in.

"Good. We'll go slow, and Blip says it isn't far."

"It is, too," Spiny said. "You'll find out."

Spiny and Blip were both right and wrong. It was not far for Dai Bando, but it was more than the girls and Bronwen had bargained for. By the time they staggered into the village of Chief Locor, they were exhausted again.

Nice round huts lined the streets of the village. Each had a small door and tiny windows. The little front lawn of each house blossomed with a multitude of different-colored flowers. Some homes had white fences lining their sidewalks; others had rock walls that had large silicon crystals built into them. The streets were narrow and very clean. And the Dulkins, all worried-looking, were bustling around their village as busy as ants. They obviously were upset about something.

"We will take you to Chief Locor," Spiny said. Then he said to Blip, "Something's going on in the village. I don't understand it."

"What is it?" Dai asked curiously.

"I don't know. There is much excitement. See how everybody is running about."

Dai and his companions followed the two Dulkins, who brought them face-to-face with a taller member of the tribe. Around his neck this man wore a gold chain with a stone of some kind that caught the light.

"Who are these strangers?" he demanded. "If they are Denebians, kill them at once!"

"They are not Denebians, Chief," Spiny told him. "As a matter of fact, I think they're running from the Denebians. But what is happening here in the village?"

Locor ignored the question. He peered up at Dai. "Who are you, and what are you doing here?"

"We're from the *Daystar*, Chief," Dai Bando said. "We're friends of Capt. Mark Edge."

Some of the suspicion was wiped from Locor's face at once. "Edge. Is he with you?"

"No, I'm afraid not."

"Too bad. He is a great warrior. We could use him."

"This is Lieutenant Jaleel, the weapons officer from our ship."

"You have weapons!" Locor cried eagerly.

"Again, I'm afraid not, Chief Locor. They were destroyed when our ship crashed. All we have are these small Neuromags."

Locor's shoulders seemed to settle. "Then we are doomed," he said.

"What's happening here, Chief?" Dai asked.

"We're being attacked by the Denebians."

"Attacked! Where are they?" Tara Jaleel cried.

"They are blasting a hole through the mountain

with their weapons. Rather than looking for entrances to our caverns, they are simply boring through."

"What will you do when they get here, Chief?" Tara Jaleel asked. "Do you have arms? How will you defend yourselves?"

Locor's face was grim. "Look around you. Do you see anything that looks like a force to stop them?"

"No." Jaleel spoke up for the rest.

"Is there no hope at all?" Dai Bando asked quickly.

"Only one," Locor said. "When Edge was here, he left a radio. But—"

"A radio!" Instantly Jerusha's eyes lit up. "Then we can contact home base!"

"—but we do not know how to use it," the chief finished.

"Well, *I* know how to use it," Jerusha cried. "Take me to the radio, Chief."

As Locor escorted Jerusha away, Dai Bando turned to Tara Jaleel. "You can see what the Lord is doing for us, Lieutenant. Jerusha will send a signal for help. There'll probably be a star cruiser here in no time to take care of the Denebians."

"We'll see," Lieutenant Jaleel said. "I won't believe it until I see it."

After watching the crash of *Daystar*, the Denebian captain signaled his second in command with a wave of his hand. His starship remained in low stationary orbit around Makon.

"Captain Koriak," his officer reported, "we've adjusted our main turbo cannons to bore a hole down through the mountain."

"Very good, Lieutenant Nakura. The tunnels on this planet are such a maze that it would take us months to find our way through them." The Denebian captain studied the remains of *Daystar* on the main viewer. What was left of the small cruiser was mostly smoking bits and pieces. "We must work quickly. That was an Intergalactic Command star cruiser, and somehow it detected us through our stealth fields. Their fleet will be on the way."

Captain Koriak was commander of the most powerful starship in Deneb space. The captain's physical presence alone commanded respect. Being seven and a half feet tall, he was head and shoulders taller than any other Denebian. His wavy hair was neck length and coal black with a few white streaks running through it. His face resembled old leather. A wide scar ran across his left cheek. Heavy eyebrows hung over coal black eyes. His skin gave off a strange green glow.

Koriak marveled at the new capabilities of his ship. Thanks to that small supply of tridium provided by Sir Richard Irons, Denebian scientists had been able to construct a cloaking device for the cruiser, as well as enhancements to its weapons and sensors.

Koriak had been under orders to learn from Sir Richard Irons the source of the tridium. Once he finally discovered that Makon was the source, that made Irons expendable. Koriak's cloaked ship then destroyed Sir Richard's *Jackray* in a surprise attack. Now he was proceeding to Makon to claim the tridium for the Denebian Empire.

Nakura was a yes-man. Koriak well knew that the lieutenant would tell him whatever he wanted to hear. Koriak considered his second in command a weasel, but a very useful weasel.

Weasels have their place, Koriak thought. *And Nakura's place is on this ship with me.* There was nothing that was said aboard the starship that Nakura didn't hear. And if Nakura heard it, Koriak would hear it, too.

"How soon do we reach the energy source?" Koriak asked as he sat in his command chair.

"If we don't run into any problems, we estimate we will bore through to a large subterranean cavern in a few hours," Nakura reported. "Our sensors have just picked up a vast body of water. The energy source appears to be coming from an island in the center of it."

"As soon as we break through, have the storm troopers dropped in. We need to assess this new power and bring it to the ship quickly."

"Aye, sir," the weasel said.

11

The Water Snake

Everywhere in the village that Dai looked, the Dulkins were scurrying around. Though a great many of them were armed, all were armed with rather simple weapons. A few had antique laser pistols, but some carried only spears and axes.

Dai found Raina helping Tara Jaleel shore up the cavern wall.

"I hope this works," she said to Dai as she lifted a heavy stone. "We have to do the best we can with what we've got. Can you lend a hand with this?"

Across the way, Tara was placing a rock in the barricade. She announced that strengthening the wall was useless. "I don't see what good this is going to do, Bando."

"I don't either, but I don't know anything else to do," Dai said.

He picked up a huge rock as if it were an enormous Ping Pong ball stuffed with Styrofoam and carried it over to her.

"You're the strongest human being I've ever seen," Raina said.

"Right now it's going to take more than muscle to stop those Denebians," Jaleel growled.

Just then a tremendous roar shook the village, and everyone looked upward.

"They're blasting through!" Tara Jaleel yelled.

Indeed it was true. A single red spot began to glow high in the cave wall. It turned white, then yellow, and then white again.

"They're burning right through with blasters!" Tara Jaleel shouted. "Get ready for them. Here they come."

Even as she yelled, the wall began to crumble and fall. Rocks shattered and showered on those who were working nearby.

"Get to cover!" Dai yelled. "They're coming!"

More and more rocks fell. Bigger and bigger rocks fell. The Dulkins ran for cover.

Dai took his station beside Tara Jaleel. They gripped their Neuromags, but he said, "I'm afraid these won't do much good, but—"

"They won't. Not for long. It's a lost cause, Bando."

"But I don't ever give up, Lieutenant." Dai smiled.

Tara Jaleel said, "Aren't you afraid?"

"Afraid? No, I'm not afraid."

"Even though you're going to die in a few minutes?"

"I don't know that, and the Lord can keep me alive if He wants me alive. Or He'll just take me to be with Him."

"You're crazy!"

"No, I'm not crazy. I just believe that the Lord is able to do anything."

A tremendous roar shook the island, the lake, and the boat that sat at its shoreline, ready to depart.

Captain Cook hesitated only seconds before screaming, "Out! Out of the boat!"

As Ringo scrambled onto land, he looked upward to the cavern ceiling. There, in front of his eyes, the silicon-imbedded rock was beginning to melt as from intense heat. In fact, the entire cavern roof was beginning to look like molten glass. Huge red-hot globules dripped into the lake, causing steam to rise from the surface.

"It has to be the Denebian cannons!" Cook cried. "They're blasting through the rock."

In minutes, the ceiling directly above Ringo turned orange, then red, and finally a bright white before that section of roof disappeared completely. Once the cannons from the Denebian starship had finished their work, he knew it would be only a little while before the Denebian storm troopers would descend upon the island. Only the intense heat from the cannons kept the invasion from happening any sooner.

"They've drilled through," he said. "Now what?"

"They'll be sending their troops in. Get ready," Captain Cook said. Her face was grim.

And that was exactly what happened. The hole became large enough for the end of a small shuttle to suddenly appear. A door swung open. Denebian troopers began pouring through it, lowering themselves on ropes. They were very quick.

"We've got to slow them down all we can," Captain Cook said and began firing.

The invaders were experts, but they couldn't have anticipated the presence of the Space Rangers and their Neuromags. After a short battle, the Denebians withdrew. However, Ringo knew they would soon be back.

"They weren't expecting us to be down here," Zeno yelled at Captain Cook. "They only planned to steal the tridium and leave."

"Poor tactics." Captain Cook scowled as she looked toward the underground lake. "Zeno, I don't see any Denebians on the surface of the water. But I know we brought down several."

Ringo glanced at the lake.

"There should be some, Captain, but I don't see any, either," the first officer said.

And then Ringo realized that something was moving about under the surface. The lake churned violently.

Ringo and Heck and Mei-Lani stood watching the swirling water with fascination. With amazing suddenness, several giant snakelike heads broke the surface. Each water snake's mouth was filled with razorlike teeth. What had happened to all of the fallen Denebians was plain to see.

A fresh unit of invaders started down the ropes. Then apparently they too saw the water snakes, for they began quickly climbing back up to the shuttle. The Denebians were withdrawing again. But now the Rangers faced another—perhaps even more deadly—enemy if they fled across the lake. The snakes.

All this time, Ringo had been aware that Heck was doing something with the heavy bag he still carried.

Suddenly Heck was yelling. "It's all right, folks. We've got a way to get out of here!"

They all gathered around him, and Heck opened his pack.

"What's that?" Ringo asked, glancing into the bag.

"I re-engineered the antigrav unit to interface with the thrusters on our envirosuits." Heck held up one of the units. It was no larger than a deck of cards.

"How did you do that?" Cook asked, at the same time eyeing the snake-filled body of water they would have to cross in their rowboat.

"I used tridium crystals. They focus power, remember," Heck explained quickly. "Plug this into your thruster control mechanism, and you become weightless. The thruster's speed will increase, making us very fast." He began showing them what to do with the antigrav device.

"This just might work," Zeno said grimly. He grabbed one, strapped it on, and the others did the same. In

110

minutes they were lifting off, powered by the antigrav units.

But when Ringo glanced back, Heck was running back up the beach. "Come on, Heck, you're going to get caught! We've got to get moving and fight them off from somewhere else."

The other Rangers began yelling at him, too.

But now Heck was at the tridium cache, clearing away the stones they had replaced on top of it.

"What's he *doing?*" Raina asked.

Ringo stared downward. "You know what I think? I think he's trying to take the tridium crystals. I'll bet his antigrav unit won't lift that much weight."

"Leave it, Heck, and come *on!*"

But Heck was scooping tridium into his pack. Ringo knew that finding the tridium was what Heck had dreamed about ever since their first mission to Makon. The tridium was his ticket to fame and fortune, and he wasn't about to let anyone, including the Denebians, take his ticket from him.

Ringo watched him. Now Heck was trying to get his antigrav unit to compensate for the added weight. He was throwing everything away except for the crystals—including his Neuromag and his communicator. Heck was so intent that he failed to notice the snake slithering up from the water toward him.

"Behind you, Heck!"

By now the other Rangers had reached the island and were yelling back at both of them. Ringo saw Heck turn around, only to come face to face with the snake. He dropped his antigrav unit and whirled to flee. To Ringo's horror, the giant snake opened its cavernous mouth and swallowed him.

He fired his Neuromag, but it was hopeless. The snake began slithering back toward the water.

"Heck!" Those watching from the island were screaming.

"I can't believe this," Ringo said when he joined them. "Heck's gone. He's gone." Tears came to his eyes.

The loss of Heck stunned all the Rangers, but Captain Cook began bellowing, "There's no time for this! Focus on the Denebians. We've got to prevent them from getting the crystals."

The first Denebian shuttle lifted off, and a second took its place. These new storm troopers were heavily armored, and each one carried a hand cannon. They were ready for a fight. Their thruster packs labored under the weight of their suits and the heavy gravity of Makon. The *Daystar* crew in their special envirosuits did not have that problem.

"Use Delta Formation Three," Cook ordered through her communicator.

The others complied immediately. This formation was like a spinning triangle, which made it hard for the attackers to hit them. Every few seconds the whirling motion of the triangle stopped, and the *Daystar* unit would fire their Neuromags.

Zeno powered himself next to the captain. "I hope Jaleel and Dai and the others are all right. Without these new antigrav units, they won't have the same advantage we do."

But Captain Cook's mind was on something else. She looked at him grimly. "I have an idea."

12
Surprise Rescue

The battle in the underground village raged furiously. What the Dulkins lacked in modern weaponry, they made up in cunning and stealth. But the Denebian weapons were deadly.

Jerusha turned just in time to see a blast strike over Dai Bando's head. It set off a shower of rocks, and one of them struck Dai, knocking him to the ground.

"Dai!" Jerusha cried. She sprang to his side and saw that he was unconscious and bleeding.

"We've got to get him out of here! Lieutenant, help me!"

Tara Jaleel ran to her, and the two began to drag Dai away from the fighting. When they found a place of relative safety, Jaleel said, "I've got to get back to the fight. See what you can do for him."

"All right."

Bending over Dai, Jerusha saw that the rock had torn a gash in his head. She took out a handkerchief and her canteen and began to wash the wound.

"Dai, can you hear me?" He did not respond, and fear raced through her. Jerusha had known for a long time that she cared for this boy, and now she knew that she cared more than she'd thought.

She took his head in her lap and held the moistened handkerchief against the wound. She did not know what else to do.

Suddenly Dai's eyes opened, and he whispered, "What happened?"

"Dai, you're all right!"

Dai Bando blinked several times and made a face. He reached up and found that she was holding the handkerchief to his head. "Something put me out," he muttered.

"A flying rock spun away from a blast and caught you right in the forehead."

"I . . . I think I'm all right."

"Don't try to move yet. Just lie there."

Dai Bando seemed content not to move. He lay still and looked up into her face. "I never told you this, Jerusha," he said quietly, "but I think you're the prettiest girl I ever saw."

Jerusha felt her face flush. She could not think of a single thing to say.

Dai waited for her to answer. When she did not reply, he said, "I've always been afraid of you, Jerusha."

"Afraid of me! But why?"

"Because you and everybody else are so talented, and all I can do is run and carry rocks and stuff. I'm not really good at anything."

"You are, too! How many times have you saved us because you're strong and courageous? What you can do *is* important."

"Do you really think so?"

"Of course, I do. I thought you knew that I did."

Dai Bando slowly sat up. He said, "I didn't know."

"Then you're not much of a judge of girls."

"I guess I'm not. I never had much practice."

The two looked at each other. He reached out suddenly and touched her cheek. "I like you better than any girl I've ever seen in my whole life."

"Do you, Dai?"

"And I've never said that to a girl before." He hesitated and then said, "I don't suppose you could ever come to like me?"

Jerusha smiled. "I think I might," she said.

Denebian command must have finally realized that their storm troopers were too slow moving to overcome the Rangers' Neuromags. Unexpectedly, the Denebian troops began to rendezvous with their shuttle.

"There they go," Ringo said, watching the green-glowing Denebians head toward their craft. "The battle's still on, but I'm glad to see *them* leaving."

Captain Cook counted her crew. "And we're still in one piece . . . except for Heck."

Thinking of Heck, swallowed by the great serpent she could still see wallowing about in the shallows below, Mei-Lani felt a great wave of sadness. Then she made herself look away and said, "Maybe the Denebians aren't as tough as we all believed."

But Captain Cook replied bleakly, "The Denebians weren't expecting any resistance. So we surprised them. That's all. The next unit of storm troopers will come down here armed to the teeth."

They watched the second shuttle lift off and head upward toward the surface.

Next, Captain Cook looked at the power setting on her Neuromag. "My power supply is down to twenty-five percent. How's everyone else?"

"I believe we all have about the same amount left, Captain," Thrax said.

And then Cook glanced down at the island shore. She frowned. "Something's going on down there. We'll check it out later. It's back to the battle for now."

The others rocketed off, but Mei-Lani and Ringo kept on staring downward. The snake that had devoured

Heck was now thrashing about wildly at the shoreline. Then she and Ringo must have had the same thought at the same time. They both swooped down toward the serpent, firing their Neuromags. In seconds, the monster fell and lay still.

"We got him, Mei-Lani!" Ringo cried.

"Yes, but look! Look what's in his teeth!"

"It's Heck! The snake wasn't able to completely swallow him!" Ringo dropped onto the shore. There he dropped his Neuromag, raced forward, and grabbed a protruding leg. He dragged Heck Jordan from the serpent's mouth and out into the light of day.

Heck was vaguely conscious of what was happening. When the lake monster seized him, he had gone into shock. The one thing he knew was that he was about to die, and the thought of death being so close was unbearable. Fear had paralyzed him.

"Are you all right, Heck?" someone kept asking over and over. "Can you speak? Heck?"

And then he realized that it was Mei-Lani. Heck sat up. He reached out and touched her as if he could not believe what he saw. "I . . . I don't know."

"Do you hurt anywhere?" Ringo was there, too. "Anything broken?"

"I . . . I don't think so."

Heck looked around wildly. "What happened? Where's the snake?"

"You were swallowed by this beast," Mei-Lani said. "I mean, it *tried* to swallow you and couldn't. That's what happened!"

Then it all came back to Heck. He began to tremble. "I thought I was going to die," he whimpered.

"You would have, if that snake could only have gotten you down its throat."

Heck turned to Ringo, and he found he still could barely talk. "I was so scared, Ringo."

"I don't blame you. Anybody would have been scared with an experience like that."

Heck was still struggling to speak. He could not express his feelings. The horror of what had happened was still on him.

"I didn't have time to think much, but I did have one thought," he gasped.

"What was that, Heck?"

"That I was going to die, and I knew I wasn't ready to die."

Ringo and Mei-Lani exchanged glances. And Heck knew what they were thinking. Both of them were aware that he had been running from God for a long time.

Mei-Lani said, "Tell him, Ringo."

Ringo Smith was as close a friend as Heck Jordan had ever had. Heck had abused him abominably and had taken advantage of him. Heck had always known that and been slightly ashamed of it. But his close experience with death made him reach out and cling to Ringo's hand. "I'm not ready to die."

"I know you're not ready, Heck," Ringo said. "Nobody is unless they know the Lord Jesus."

"What do I do? Tell me. I'll do anything."

"The first thing you must do," Ringo said, "is simply admit that you've sinned—that you haven't pleased God."

"Oh, man, I've always known that."

"No, you haven't, Heck. Not really. You've been bragging all your life about what a great guy you are."

Heck closed his eyes and swallowed hard. "Well, I know it now," he said, and two tears suddenly formed. "I couldn't help the bragging. I felt so awful. I was always so fat, and I was ashamed, so I had to brag to cover it up."

"You don't have to do that with the Lord," Ringo said quietly. "He knows all about you—every thought you ever had."

"And that scares me, because I've had some really bad thoughts."

"You can never disappoint God, Heck."

Heck frowned. "What do you mean, I can't disappoint Him? I disappoint Him all the time."

"I mean you can only disappoint somebody when they expect one thing and you do something else. Something bad. But God already *knows* what you're going to do. Always. He knows that all of us do bad stuff. He can be grieved, but He can't be disappointed."

Heck thought on that. "I know I've sinned, all right," he muttered finally. "I've stolen things, I've lied, and I've been a big blowhard—just tell me what to do."

Heck listened closely as Ringo and Mei-Lani explained how he could be forgiven. Then he said wonderingly, "Is that all there is to it?"

"Listen, Heck," Ringo said, "the Bible says that if you know you're a sinner and if you believe that the Lord Jesus is the One God sent to save you, you can ask Him to forgive you, and He will. And then, the Bible says you are in God's family forever!"

Heck straightened up. "Can I ask Him right now?"

"You can ask Him right now."

The three prayed then, first Mei-Lani and then Ringo. And finally Heck gasped out a prayer for himself.

"You know what, Heck?" Mei-Lani said when he finished. "You've got a lot of brothers and sisters now. And we all love you." She reached over and patted his hand.

118

Heck Jordan's throat was full. He knew that danger still lay ahead, but he also knew that what he was hearing was the truth. "I don't see why you guys ever put up with me," he muttered. "I don't see why God put up with me."

Ringo said quietly, "But we all feel that way, Heck." The noise of battle grew louder, and he said, "Why don't you stay here with Heck for a few minutes more, Mei-Lani? Until he's doing better. I'll go see what's going on."

"I'll do that," Mei-Lani said. "All right, Heck?"

"Sure. I'm still a little bit shaky. But if you'll stay with me, I'll be fine."

13
Decision in the Tunnel

Never had Tara Jaleel, the weapons officer, fled from anything or turned her back on the enemy. And it was like her never to let anyone else know that she had a weakness. So she had never told anybody that she had a secret fear of being underground. She had even laughed and taunted Mei-Lani about *her* fears. But deep down, there was this terrible, agonizing dread that she kept well under guard.

Tara and her companions had reached a part of the underground kingdom of the Dulkins that lay in darkness. The fluorescent rock seemed to have run out, and now they had only the light from their hand-held electronic torches. In the dimness of the cavern tunnel, her courage oozed out completely. Tara Jaleel began to run.

I've got to get out of here! she thought. *I can't stand this tunnel any longer!*

"What was that?"

Raina and Bronwen were trailing well behind Tara Jaleel. Dai Bando and Jerusha brought up the rear.

"It sounded like Tara," Bronwen said.

"Maybe she's run into some kind of trouble. Let's catch up with her."

Raina and Bronwen raced ahead through the dark tunnel by the glow of their electronic flashlights. And then Raina could clearly hear Tara Jaleel calling.

"What could be wrong?" Bronwen exclaimed. "I just can't see much with these little lights."

Raina shook her head. "I don't know, but she wouldn't call out like that if she weren't in bad trouble," she said. *"Bronwen, watch out!"*

They halted, and it was well they did, for in front of them the tunnel floor simply dropped away!

"Don't fall off that!" Raina cried.

She frowned at the edge of the sudden drop-off. Then she picked up a stone and tossed it over. She waited for what seemed a long time before hearing a small *plink*. Obviously the hole was deep.

"She couldn't have come this way . . ." Bronwen said, puzzled. "And yet we heard her. Where—"

"If she fell off, she's lost forever."

And then a feeble cry arose from somewhere below them. "I'm here. Help . . . help me! I'm here."

"That's Tara!" Bronwen cried. "She's down there somewhere!"

They both got on their hands and knees then, crept to the rim, and looked over.

"There she is!" Raina gasped.

Tara Jaleel was in a terrible position. She was balancing herself on a ledge not far down, hanging onto another outcrop by her fingers. Her eyes stared upward at them and were wide with fear.

"Help me!" she pleaded. "I can't hold on much longer."

"Take my flashlight. I'm going down to see if I can help her," Raina said, swinging a foot over the side. "There are some rocks sticking out to give me a foothold. Keep shining the light on us."

"Be careful, Raina. Anything could happen here."

Carefully Raina slid backward over the edge of the

crevasse. Just beneath her now was the narrow rock shelf that Tara Jaleel was desperately clutching.

"Help me, please!" Tara moaned.

"I'm coming. Hang on."

If Mei-Lani was afraid of darkness, Raina St. Clair was afraid of heights. She always had been, ever since she was a little girl. She knew she could not do this in her own strength, and she prayed aloud, "Jesus, help *me!*"

Then she began making a cautious descent to the ledge Tara Jaleel clung to.

Suddenly everything began to shake.

"What's that?" she cried out.

"It must be the Denebians trying to blast through," Bronwen said from above her. "Can you reach her?"

"Not yet. But almost. I'm going to try."

Raina reached downward and found that she could barely touch Tara's fingertips.

At that moment the weapons officer began to call out fiercely, "Save me, Shiva!"

But her idol goddess did not answer.

Raina glanced upward. "Bronwen! Quick! Go get Dai!"

"I'll be back as soon as I can. He and Jerusha were right behind us."

Raina tried again but could not reach Tara. The weapons officer was becoming distraught, and Raina could not think what to do. She prayed fervently, and then a thought came to her.

With one hand she whipped off her leather belt and buckled one end tightly about the other wrist. Then she lowered the belt toward Jaleel. "Tara, grab this! I'll pull you up onto the ledge."

But Tara Jaleel seemed paralyzed with fear. "I can't let go!"

"You've got to let go. Grab the belt! It's your only hope!"

Tara kept on calling upon Shiva, but now her fingers were slipping. Finally, in a desperate gesture, she reached out a hand and seized Raina's belt. Then she caught it with her other hand as well.

"Don't let me fall, Raina!" she pleaded. "Please don't!"

"The only One that can help us now is the Lord Jesus," Raina said. She pulled upward, trying to lift Tara's weight. Now the ground was shaking even more.

"I don't want to fall into that black hole! Don't drop me!"

"I'll never drop you," Raina promised. "I'll never let go."

But Tara's weight was pulling Raina forward, and Jaleel cried out, "We're falling!"

"No, we're not."

Raina held on grimly. She shut her eyes and prayed—but she could still feel herself sliding, sliding off the narrow ledge.

She knew Tara Jaleel had unusual strength for a woman. She could hold on. But Raina St. Clair also knew, as she clung to a rock with one hand as the belt cut into her other wrist, that she was slowly being dragged toward the edge. She felt her strength rapidly playing out. She gritted her teeth and prayed, "Oh, Lord, I'm not strong, but You are. Help me to hold her. And send Dai soon!"

Dangling over the darkness, Tara Jaleel, in spite of her fear, still found herself thinking, *This girl is willing to die herself to save me!* She had treated Raina— indeed, all the Rangers—so badly. She had insulted her, had done everything she could to humiliate and embarrass her. And still, looking up into the girl's pale face, she knew that Raina St. Clair would die sooner than let her go.

"Hang on, friend. You won't fall. God will help us." Hearing Raina call her "friend" brought a lump to Tara Jaleel's throat. No one had ever called her that. She suddenly knew what love was. "Good-bye, Raina. I love you." It was the first time she had ever admitted to loving anybody.

"*Don't let go!* Help is coming!" Raina cried.

Tara saw Raina sliding forward until nearly half her body was off the narrow shelf. But then at that moment a strong hand reached down and seized the belt.

"Dai!" Raina choked.

"Take it easy, Raina. You're all right now."

With a burst of his tremendous strength, Dai lifted both Raina and Tara Jaleel straight upward.

Tara could scarcely take in what was happening. Dai Bando was lifting them both with one hand. Then she was planting her feet at the edge of the drop-off and gratefully whispering, "Thank you, Dai." She could say no more.

"Careful now," Dai Bando said. He swung them toward Jerusha, who drew them away from the edge.

"Are you all right, Lieutenant?" Jerusha asked.

Tara Jaleel could not answer. She could only nod.

"Here. Let me get you farther back, where you'll be safe." Dai scooped up Tara and took her to Bronwen. Then he knelt beside them. "Are you all right?" he asked.

Tears were running down Tara Jaleel's cheeks. "I don't know when I've ever cried before. Not since I was a child."

"It's all right to cry," Bronwen said. "I do it myself sometimes."

"Raina"—Tara looked up at the ensign—"you would have died to save me, wouldn't you?"

Bronwen said, "There was Another who did die to save you." She continued to speak of Jesus, while the two girls and Dai listened.

Then Dai Bando knelt again beside the weapons officer. "All you have to do is let go, Lieutenant. Let go of trusting anything other than just Jesus. Will you do that?"

"But what if it doesn't work?"

"Trusting Jesus always works," he said confidently. "Doesn't it, Aunt?"

"Jesus will never fail us. 'The one who comes to me I will certainly not cast out.' He said that Himself, while He was here on earth."

"But you don't know how awful I've been. You've seen some of the terrible things I've done, but you don't know everything."

"We're all sinners, my dear. Just call upon Him. He's waiting to forgive you."

And right there in the Dulkins' tunnel on the planet Makon, Tara Jaleel, the toughest weapons officer in the galaxy, gave her heart to Jesus Christ.

14
The Tridium

Captain Cook rocketed up to the blasted-open entrance in the ceiling of the cave and looked out. "No one's coming yet," she told the others over the intercom.

Then she looked downward at the island. So Heck Jordan was safe after all. She was glad for that. But there he sat beside his tridium cache. She knew what must be done. The boy was a victim of his own greed. No one person should be allowed possession of those precious crystals.

She took out her datacorder and tried to get a more accurate reading of the lake's depth. But her device could measure down only fifty miles. *One thing is for sure,* Cook thought, *between the snakes and the depth of this lake, no one will be able to retrieve the tridium when I finish with it. Those crystals will be gone forever.*

Next, the captain ordered the bridge crew to rendezvous at the tridium cache. "I think we have only a few moments before the next attack. As I told you, I have an idea that may just stop hostilities."

"And what is that, Captain?" Zeno Thrax asked.

"The crystals," she said. "We must get rid of the crystals."

Zeno looked thoughtful. "That may be a good idea."

"Well, *I* don't think it's a good idea!" Heck cried. "Tridium is the future of the galaxy! We might even be able to harness tridium and travel to another galaxy at speeds that are unimaginable to us now. Besides, I found them!"

"Don't give us that, Heck," Ringo interrupted. "I don't buy into bright ideas anymore. These crystals came very close to ending your life. You have to let them go."

"But listen—if Intergalactic Command has the tridium, then we won't have to fear the Denebians anymore. We would be more powerful than they are. More powerful than anybody."

Cook jumped in. "Heck, the Denebians would never rest if they believed Intergalactic Command had the means to destroy them. The best thing to do right now is dump the crystals into the lake. That way, no one will have them. The balance of power between the Denebians and Intergalactic Command would then remain as it is now." She looked around at the others. "We've got some important things to worry about, so gather round. This is my plan . . ."

On the bridge of the Denebian starship, Captain Koriak was enraged. "This was supposed to be a simple mission, Nakura! And now you're telling me that we have lost most of the men in the second and third contingents?"

Nakura feared for his life. "Captain, our men fought gallantly, but we were surprised by the Intergalactic Command troops. There were thousands of them on the island. Our soldiers fought bravely, but we were outnumbered by a hundred to one."

Koriak eyed him suspiciously.

"Their thrusters are much faster than ours. They raced around so fast that it seemed our men were flying motionless. They would fly over our heads, and we'd fire at them with our cannons and strike nothing but the cave ceiling. Huge rocks would rain down on our men, killing them." Nakura was wringing his hands. "And the creatures, Captain. There are man-eating snakes on that island. Many of our men were eaten alive."

"Prepare contingents four, five, and six."

"Aye, Captain." Nakura sighed.

"Make sure they are fully armed. And put boosters on the thruster packs."

"Aye, Captain." Nakura signaled to his aide with a nod of his head.

"Have the fourth contingent battle the Intergalactic Command troops. Assign the fifth contingent to destroy the snakes. And have the sixth contingent retrieve the energy source."

"Aye, Captain."

"And Nakura . . ."

Nakura stood silent, looking down at the deck.

"Don't fail me this time, or it will cost you your life!"

"I can't believe we're doing this," Heck wailed.

"No other choice," Ringo replied matter-of-factly.

Captain Cook divided the cache of crystals equally among the Rangers, Zeno Thrax, and herself. The thruster packs could easily handle the lighter loads of tridium.

Cook's voice sounded on their communicators. "Follow me," she ordered.

They all flew behind her out over the lake, each holding his package of crystals.

"Now, dump the crystals out of the bags," she commanded.

Below them, the surface of the water churned

with the great snakes. Occasionally one would leap upward, but they maintained a high enough altitude to stay out of reach of their gaping mouths. The released tridium plummeted toward the lake like so much salt being poured out of a box. The churning water threw the crystals in every direction, and then they sank below the surface.

"It will take them a while to sink to the bottom. I don't think there *is* a bottom to it," the captain said.

"None?" Mei-Lani asked.

"There must be. But my datacorder only scans down to fifty miles, and this lake is deeper than that." Cook held out the datacorder in front of her. "There. The tridium energy signal has dissipated. Now let's get out of this cavern."

She led her crew to the opening in the ceiling, and they began their ascent to the surface.

Koriak stood in disbelief. Two things had happened at the same time. The energy signature had disappeared, and his long-range sensors had scanned four Magnum Deep Space Cruisers headed toward the planet. They looked to be fully armed.

"Recall the troops immediately," Koriak ordered.

"Captain?" Nakura obviously did not understand the seriousness of the situation.

"The energy signature is gone. I don't understand why. It just disappeared," Koriak said as he twisted dials.

"Maybe we can relocate it after our men get down into the cavern."

"You're an idiot, Nakura. The men will find nothing. The energy signature is gone."

"But, Captain, if we don't retrieve the energy source, how will you explain the loss of our men?"

"You let me worry about that. A fleet of Intergalactic Command star cruisers is headed this way! Depart for Denebian space just as soon as the last unit of troops arrives."

"Aye, Captain."

"They've left," Jerusha told Tara Jaleel. "Believe it or not. All of them."

"Left?"

"All the Denebian storm troopers went back to their ship." Jerusha read her datacorder. Then she adjusted two dials. "Now the starship is moving out of orbit."

"What kind of warriors *are* these Denebians?" Tara Jaleel sneered. "They come here, start a fight, and then take off without victory. Where's the honor in that?"

"I think," Bronwen spoke up, "that they aren't running from *us*, Tara."

"Of course! The fleet!" Raina interjected. "The fleet is on the way. Our signal got through after all."

"The Denebian ship by itself could not defeat a fleet of Intergalactic Command Deep Space Cruisers," the navigator continued. "It's the only thing that makes sense. There is no reason for them to run from *us*."

Everyone cheered.

To Jerusha it seemed forever before they were out into full daylight again. Dai's group brought Chief Locor with them to the surface of Makon. There the bridge crew happily joined them, and everyone stood for a while without talking, just looking over the remains of *Daystar*. The cruiser had exploded into a thousand tiny pieces and looked rather like a metallic rug carpeting the ground.

The chief rubbed his head. "I could never have told that this was once a star cruiser. It looks like so much rubble now."

The Space Rangers could only bow their heads in sorrow. They had lost everything. Except for their battle gear, all they owned had been aboard the ship when it exploded.

Zeno was reading his datacorder. "The Denebians fired on her with their turbo cannons. That, combined with the damage that she had already sustained, caused the explosion. Well, we'll never forget the *Daystar*."

Jerusha watched the first officer shake his head in disbelief. She knew Zeno Thrax had come to love this ship and her crew.

She pushed at some of the debris with her foot. "And we'll never, never forget Ivan, and Studs, and the grunts," she said sadly.

"Won't forget *who?*" a voice said behind her.

Jerusha whirled and saw only empty air. She then felt something poking her kneecap.

Ivan Petroski was standing right next to her, looking straight up. Then he turned to Captain Cook. "Captain, we are all alive and well." The dwarf pointed to the heavy forest, and Jerusha saw Studs and the grunts approaching from the far end of the valley.

"We hid in the forest," the chief engineer explained. "There was no way for us to enter the tunnels while the Denebians were firing their turbo cannons. We felt helpless. The Denebian shuttles could fly right into the tunnels they drilled, but those openings were so high on the mountain that it would have taken us a week to hike up that far."

Cook looked at the mountaintop. It was still smoking from the Denebian assault.

Suddenly Chief Locor chuckled. "And Captain Edge was indeed right."

"About what?" Jerusha asked.

"Edge told me a saying that he had heard—about all things working to the good. I forget the rest of it."

" 'And we know that God causes all things to work together for good to those who love God.' It's a Bible verse. One of my favorites," Raina said. "But it's talking about what God does for His own people."

"I expect Edge didn't remember all of that," Locor said. "But it certainly is true in our case." He chuckled again.

"What do you mean, Chief?" Bronwen asked.

"If I were to choose two places to bore tunnels into the mountain, I couldn't have picked two better places. One tunnel to the village, and one to the underground lake." He looked at the mountaintop. "We needed better ventilation shafts, and now we have them. It would have taken several centuries for us to accomplish what the Denebians did in a day with their turbo cannons."

Cook spoke up then. "I'm sure, Chief Locor, that Intergalactic Command will do everything possible to help you improve Makon."

Perseus, the flagship of Intergalactic Command, gracefully arced down from orbit and landed on a flat area several hundred yards from Captain Cook and her crew. At a nod from her, the Rangers raced forward to meet the ship, leaving the older officers and the grunts to approach at a slower pace.

When the huge gangway of the Magnum Deep Space Cruiser was lowered to the ground in front of them, Commandant Lee herself was the first person down. She hugged each Ranger.

"I am so proud of you," the commandant said. "We were expecting a fierce battle, but no battle will be fought by us today. The Denebian starship had already hightailed it from Makon before we arrived." She smiled warmly. "Our other cruisers are following the Denebians to make sure they return to Deneb."

"Commandant, did you *see* that ship? I've never seen anything like it," Ringo said energetically.

"Neither have I," she said. "And I'm sure that neither have any of our scientists. They will be eager to get as much information as they can about it."

"I'd sure like to know what they find out," Heck said.

"I believe you'll have that opportunity, Heck. Perhaps sooner than you think."

"Commandant," Bronwen said, "I perceive that you have something in mind."

The commandant laughed aloud. "I could never hide anything from you, Bronwen." She looked around at the *Daystar* Space Rangers. "Each of you has been upgraded to the rank of ensign in Intergalactic Command service. You will be receiving your new orders in a few days."

Every Ranger's mouth hung open in disbelief. Could it be true? Something each one had dreamed of was now actually happening. They were full-fledged Intergalactic Command Rangers. They wouldn't be considered kids anymore. All six exploded in a cheer.

15

The New Ringo

Raina St. Clair had been walking by herself for a long time. Now she took a deep breath, enjoying the fresh air and the new day that had just begun at Command Base Three. She much preferred life in the open outdoors. She always said that everything just seemed more alive outside.

She strolled along pathways lined at times by green trees and green grass. Something that she could not identify was disturbing her this morning. It was a puzzling sort of thing.

Singing began overhead, and she looked upward to see a beautifully colored bird sitting in the branches. She paused while he poured his heart out in melodious song. "You must know something that I don't to be able to sing like that."

The bird sang a few more notes, then cocked his head and looked at her as if to say, "Well, why don't you find out what it is?"

Raina smiled at the bird and then continued her walk.

The mission to Makon had taken a great deal out of all of them. Still, she was unusually depressed. "What's wrong with me?" she muttered. "We all got back safely. No one was hurt. I ought to be singing like that bird back there."

But she could not find it in her heart to rejoice. Down the path she walked. She came to a quiet stream then, and for a time she sat beside it, watching the silvery minnows glitter when the sun struck their scales. She wondered how they could all move at the same instant. As she watched, a group of several hundred changed direction at the same moment and shot away, stirring up the golden sand that formed the bottom of the stream. *Not even spaceships can move like that,* she thought.

Still feeling rather drained, Raina got up and made her way back toward the *Perseus.* As she did, she saw two figures walking together up ahead. Then the figures stood still. Raina saw that it was Jerusha and Dai, and they were holding hands. And at that moment Raina recognized why she was so depressed.

She watched as the two walked along together. Now Jerusha was looking at Dai and laughing. Raina found herself even more depressed. The truth of it all seemed a bitter pill for her to swallow.

For a long time now, Raina St. Clair had day-dreamed about Dai Bando. There had been a time when she was even jealous of Jerusha, whom Dai obviously favored. It had been a struggle, but she had thought that she was over it. Still, the sight of the two of them so happy together did not cheer her spirits.

"They look like a happy pair, don't they?"

Startled, Raina turned. Ringo had come up behind her. He was wearing a freshly pressed Ranger uniform, and she noticed how much he had matured since the first time they served together on the *Daystar.* She also noticed again that there was a new confidence about Ringo. Doubt and fear had been replaced with faith and strength. The change in him amazed her, but she liked it.

Remembering his question, she said, "Yes, they do look happy."

"They're real special people," Ringo said quietly. Then he asked, "Been out for a walk?"

"Yes, I went down to the little stream."

"Stream? I haven't seen that yet."

Raina had wanted to be alone, but now found that she did not. She said quickly, "I'll show it to you."

Raina and Ringo walked back to the stream and followed the path alongside it. The sun was going higher every moment, and a warm breeze ruffled the quiet waters.

"I wonder if there are any fish in here?" Raina asked idly.

"It looks fishy to me. Maybe we can get some poles and try it sometime."

"I'd . . . like that," Raina said.

Ringo gave her a quick glance. "You're feeling a little bit left out, aren't you?"

"I don't know what makes you say that."

"Well, maybe it's because I feel the same way myself."

Raina could not answer, but she was fascinated by Ringo's insight. "You never used to notice things like that," she said.

"I guess not. But I'm noticing a lot of things now."

"Noticing things like what?"

"Well," Ringo paused and studied her face. "I'm noticing how you have a few little freckles across your nose."

"I do not!" Raina's hand flew up, and her eyes opened wide in protest.

He laughed. "No, you don't. I was just teasing."

"Shame on you, Ringo Smith."

"But I have been noticing other things—like how grown up you've gotten lately."

Raina smiled. "I guess we all have."

"You're looking more and more like . . . like a grown-up woman." He hesitated, then added, "And a pretty one, too."

It was the first compliment that Ringo had ever paid her, and Raina felt herself blushing. She could not think of an answer. Finally she said again, almost defensively, "Well, we're *all* growing up."

Then Ringo said, "I think the Rangers won't be together much longer as a team."

"Why shouldn't we be?" she asked quickly.

"Oh, I've been hearing talk. That we're going to be given new jobs. Split up and put on different Intergalactic Command ships."

"I don't like that. I was hoping we'd all be assigned to the same ship again." Then she said, "But I shouldn't complain. It's the Lord who really controls what happens in our lives, and He always does what is right."

"Command doesn't want us to become too dependent on one another, they say. They want to see how we can function with different crews."

"But we've been doing so well. We've had so many successful missions . . ."

"That's true, but things change. By the way, I hear Captain Edge has been made the captain of a Magnum Deep Space Cruiser. We probably won't be flying with him anymore. They say he'll be directing the show in the Omega Quadrant."

"He'll like that. Omega is very deep in uncharted space, and Captain Edge loves a challenge."

"I think he'd like anything as long as he's got Dr. Cole with him."

"Were you surprised when they got married?" she asked.

"I was. They seemed to fight all the time when she first came on board."

Raina made a face. "Well, the course of true love never did run smooth."

Ringo stared at her. "You make that up?"

"Of course not. I read it in a poem somewhere or other. I forget which one."

"Well, the course of true love is running smooth now for those two."

They sat down on an old log and watched the stream for a while. A fish would break the water every now and then. Raina kept stealing glances at Ringo. She remembered how uncertain he had been when he first came on board the *Daystar*. She remembered how he kept to himself and seemed so shy that it was painful. And now she was seeing a new Ringo Smith, strong and confident. He even seemed taller. Finally she said, "I guess you're growing up, too, Ringo. I can tell."

He met her eyes, and she smiled at him.

Then he reached over and took her hand. "I guess we'll just keep on growing up and see where we go from here."

"That would be fine, Ringo."

After a while they started back to the *Perseus*. A change had taken place, Raina knew, and they would never again be as they had been before.

16

On to the Future

The *Perseus* plowed through space, shooting past galaxies like a single pulse of light.

Inside the spaceship, a party was going on. It was Heck Jordan's idea. He'd kept insisting, "We've got to have a party! After all, we'll be breaking up when we get back to Earth. We'll never all be together again. And we're important to each other." Heck had been behaving like a new person since he found the Lord.

The word came down to them from Captain Cook herself. She'd called the new Intergalactic Command ensigns together and said, "This may be unpleasant news, but now that the *Daystar* is gone, you will of course receive new assignments. And it's not likely that you'll all be serving together. Be prepared for that."

"We know," Ringo replied gloomily. "The rumors run wild even on a Magnum Cruiser."

Captain Cook herself had changed greatly since their experience on Makon. There was a gentleness in her that had never been there before. Not only the Rangers but also the rest of the crew knew it.

She ended her announcement by saying, "Sometimes it takes some pretty rough shaking up to bring us to ourselves. I've learned a lot from you Space Rangers, and from the rest of the crew as well. I will be a better officer because of it."

Every Ranger hastened to assure Captain Cook that she had performed nobly on the mission. And it was then that Heck had said, "We've got to have a going-away party, Captain. It may be our last chance."

Even Captain Cook agreed, and she ordered the cooks to cooperate by providing anything in the galley for the celebration.

So all of the Rangers and the remaining crew of the *Daystar* were gathered in the *Perseus*'s large recreation area. The only two friends who were missing were Captain Edge and the new Mrs. Edge, the former Dr. Temple Cole.

By now all the Rangers had received their new assignments. Along with Tara Jaleel, Dai Bando was being assigned to the new *Livingstone*. They would be in charge of all the physical training and martial arts programs on that cruiser. Jerusha Ericson was to be the chief engineer aboard Captain Edge's ship. She was very happy about that surprise assignment but was upset that she and Dai would be apart for so long. They agreed to leave their futures in the Lord's hands.

Raina and Ringo were both posted to Command Base Three. Raina would work in Communications and Ringo in Main Computer Control. These were serious assignments, considering the ongoing threat of the Denebians. Ringo and Raina looked forward to seeing each other often at their new location.

Mei-Lani was to be the historical and linguistic officer, working directly under Captain Cook aboard the newly refitted *Cromwell*. The captain now seemed to think of Mei-Lani almost as a daughter. It was an affection that Mei-Lani felt for the captain, too.

Last, but not least, Heck Jordan had been assigned to Intergalactic Command itself. His genius at electronics design was vital to the future of intergalactic space. As a result of this important assignment, Ringo declared with a smile, Heck's head was almost as big as his body. Even with the Lord living inside Heck Jordan, mastering his pride was going to be a challenge.

Ringo was talking with Raina when Heck raised his voice to get the attention of the old *Daystar* crew and everyone else. "All right, now," he announced, "it's program time. Everybody take a seat."

Chuckling at Heck's normal bossiness, everyone sat. Ringo and Raina found a place by Ivan Petroski. Ringo glanced at Ivan. As usual, the little engineer's short legs were dangling off his chair, something that Ringo knew irritated him no end.

"Get on with it," Ivan grumbled.

Heck started his speech. "As you all know—" he cleared his throat "—when Captain Cook was made captain of *Daystar*, she started a series of tests designed to reveal our already well-known weaknesses."

Everyone laughed, including Captain Cook.

"After many hours of serious research, I have discovered that one of us, a certain chief engineer who shall remain nameless, almost started a mutiny among the crew members that were assigned to our cargo hold—namely the grunts."

The grunts, led by Myron, clapped enthusiastically.

Heck continued. "This chief engineer can orchestrate Star Drive engines to the point of perfection. But human beings—now there's another story altogether."

Ringo watched Ivan fidgeting. Ivan was in for trouble. Heck Jordan was an expert at trouble.

"Myron," Heck said next, "if you'll please bring in the package . . ."

Myron got up from his place and brought a bulky package to Heck. He set it on the deck before him. "I hope you know what you're doing," the grunt said, loud enough for mostly everyone to hear.

Heck winked at him. Slowly he began undoing the wrapping about the package.

When the wrapping fell away, the entire roomful of people gasped—except for Ivan Petroski. Ivan jumped off his chair. He planted both feet on the floor. His fists were on his hips. "What's the meaning of this?" he demanded.

It was a robot the same height as Ivan. Its face even resembled Ivan's, and Heck had dressed it in some of Ivan's clothes. Then Heck flipped a switch on the mechanical man.

The robot began speeding from person to person, barking order after order. It raced so fast it was hard to follow with the eyes. So many orders were given that it would have been impossible to remember them all, much less carry them out.

The whole recreation hall was in tears from laughter, for the robot sounded—and acted—just like Ivan.

When the mechanical man came to Heck, it said, "Hi, handsome, you look good today." The next time it passed him, it said. "Heck, I wish I were as brilliant as you." Finally, the robot reached Heck for the third time. This time it said, "Your wish is my command."

By now, Ivan practically had smoke coming out of his ears. It appeared that he had all he could stand. He ran toward the robot. Clearly, he was going to put a stop to this.

The robot screamed. It began racing about the room. Ivan Petroski chased it.

"*H-e-l-p!*" the robot cried. "Save me! Let me alone, or I'll mutiny" were the last words the robot said before Ivan tackled it and knocked it to the deck.

With its final mechanical breath, the robot looked at Ivan and said, "Give us a kiss." And then Heck's invention powered down to lifelessness.

The roar of laughter was too much for even Ivan, and finally the chief engineer began laughing himself. Then he picked up the robot and walked over to Heck. "Heck Jordan," he said, "I'll never forget you as long as I live."

Still grinning broadly, Ringo said, "And, Heck, neither will we."

Get swept away in the many Gilbert Morris Adventures available from Moody Press:

"Too Smart" Jones

4025-8 Pool Party Thief
4026-6 Buried Jewels
4027-4 Disappearing Dogs
4028-2 Dangerous Woman
4029-0 Stranger in the Cave
4030-4 Cat's Secret
4031-2 Stolen Bicycle
4032-0 Wilderness Mystery
4033-9 Spooky Mansion
4034-7 Mysterious Artist

Come along for the adventures and mysteries Juliet "Too Smart" Jones always manages to find. She and her other homeschool friends solve these great adventures and learn biblical truths along the way. Ages 9-14

Seven Sleepers - The Lost Chronicles

3667-6 The Spell of the Crystal Chair
3668-4 The Savage Game of Lord Zarak
3669-2 The Strange Creatures of Dr. Korbo
3670-6 City of the Cyborgs
3671-4 The Temptations of Pleasure Island
3672-2 Victims of Nimbo

More exciting adventures from the Seven Sleepers. As these exciting young people attempt to faithfully follow Goél, they learn important moral and spiritual lessons. Come along with them as they encounter danger, intrigue, and mystery. Ages 10-14

MOODY
The Name You Can Trust
1-800-678-8812 www.MoodyPress.org

Dixie Morris Animal Adventures

Follow the exciting adventures of this animal lover as she learns more of God and His character through her many adventures underneath the Big Top. Ages 9-14

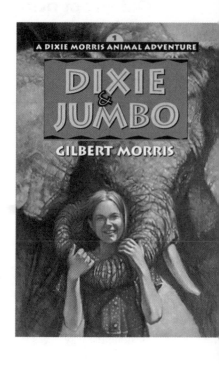

The Daystar Voyages

Join the crew of the Daystar as they traverse the wide expanse of space. Adventure and danger abound, but they learn time and again that God is truly the Master of the Universe. Ages 10-14

MOODY
The Name You Can Trust
1-800-678-8812 www.MoodyPress.org

Seven Sleepers Series

3681-1　Flight of the Eagles
3682-X　The Gates of Neptune
3683-3　The Swords of Camelot
3684-6　The Caves That Time Forgot
3685-4　Winged Riders of the Desert
3686-2　Empress of the Underworld
3687-0　Voyage of the Dolphin
3691-9　Attack of the Amazons
3692-7　Escape with the Dream Maker
3693-5　The Final Kingdom

Go with Josh and his friends as they are sent by Goél, their spiritual leader, on dangerous and challenging voyages to conquer the forces of darkness in the new world. Ages 10-14

Bonnets and Bugles Series

0911-3　Drummer Boy at Bull Run
0912-1　Yankee Bells in Dixie
0913-X　The Secret of Richmond
　　　　　Manor
0914-8　The Soldier Boy's Discovery
0915-6　Blockade Runner
0916-4　The Gallant Boys of
　　　　　Gettysburg
0917-2　The Battle of Lookout
　　　　　Mountain
0918-0　Encounter at Cold Harbor
0919-9　Fire Over Atlanta
0920-2　Bring the Boys Home

Follow good friends Leah Carter and Jeff Majors as they experience danger, intrigue, compassion, and love in these civil war adventures. Ages 10-14

MOODY
The Name You Can Trust
1-800-678-8812 www.MoodyPress.org

Moody Press, a ministry of the Moody Bible Institute,
is designed for education, evangelization, and edification.
If we may assist you in knowing more about Christ
and the Christian life, please write us without obligation:
Moody Press, c/o MLM, Chicago, Illinois 60610.